Packaged Lives

CW00954331

Middle East Literature in Translation
Michael Beard *and* Adnan Haydar, *Series Editors*

Packaged Lives

Ten Stories
and a Novella

Haifa Zangana

Selected by
Mundher Adhami
and Wen-chin Ouyang

Translated from the Arabic by
Wen-chin Ouyang

Syracuse University Press

Copyright © 2021 by Wen-chin Ouyang

Syracuse University Press

Syracuse, New York 13244-5290

All Rights Reserved

First Edition 2021

21 22 23 24 25 26   6 5 4 3 2 1

∞ The paper used in this publication meets the minimum requirements
of the American National Standard for Information Sciences—Permanence
of Paper for Printed Library Materials, ANSI Z39.48-1992.

For a listing of books published and distributed by Syracuse University Press,
visit https://press.syr.edu.

ISBN: 978-0-8156-1137-0 (paperback)
       978-0-8156-5541-1 (e-book)

Library of Congress Cataloging-in-Publication Data

Names: Zangana, Haifa, 1950– author. | Adhami, Mundher, editor. |
    Ouyang, Wen-chin, translator.

Title: Packaged lives : ten stories and a novella / Haifa Zangana ; selected by
    Mundher Adhami and Wen-chin Ouyang ; translated from the Arabic by
    Wen-chin Ouyang.

Description: First edition. | Syracuse, New York : Syracuse University Press,
    2021. | Series: Middle East literature in translation | Summary: "'Packaged
    Lives' is a collection of ten short stories and a novella, originally written in
    Arabic, by Iraqi-Kurdish writer Haifa Zangana"— Provided by publisher.

Identifiers: LCCN 2021016163 (print) | LCCN 2021016164 (ebook) |
    ISBN 9780815611370 (paperback) | ISBN 9780815655411 (ebook)

Subjects: LCGFT: Short stories. | Novellas.

Classification: LCC PJ7876.A647 P33 2021 (print) | LCC PJ7876.A647 (ebook) |
    DDC 892.7/36—dc23

LC record available at https://lccn.loc.gov/2021016163

LC ebook record available at https://lccn.loc.gov/2021016164

Manufactured in the United States of America

For Lun-Yun Chang

張龍雲

To Friendship

Contents

Introduction

Michael Beard

We go on tours to make memories, or so we are told. It's part of the package. Often enough the places we visit have memories of their own. At our best, we learn from the memory of the place, its history and values. In the title novella it is a hike to St. Patrick's Grave. By implication the conflict-ridden history of Catholic Ireland is under there. In "Pilgrimages" it is a tour of the village in Wales where Dylan Thomas was born. It centers not on his house but the public space where his poem "The Hunchback in the Park" is set. The poem, one of Thomas's most melancholy, is about the sad memory of a homeless man who is tormented and abused there. If you want to find evidence of painful memories you can find them everywhere. The experience of a tour may show you in miniature the relation between an individual and history. For some privileged people, history is seen at a distance. And some have experienced it up close.

Most of her readers will know Haifa Zangana as one of our most astute political observers, with a formidable list of indispensable writings. (There are books, research, and opinion pieces in the *Guardian* and *Al-Ahram Weekly* and interviews in print and on the radio. She does research for the United Nations Economic and Social Commission for Western Asia and is a founding member of the International Association of Contemporary Iraqi Studies.) As an Iraqi Kurd, she is a particularly keen observer of cruel fissures in her culture.

It is terrible to say that so many of those who have read her know her first from her experience as a prisoner in Saddam Hussein's Iraq. Her writings have the authority of conceptual precision and passionate commitment, but also the authority of having been there, of knowing history from the painful inside. It is possible to have seen too much history.

She was in her teens during Saddam Hussein's rise to power, at a time when Iraq was not on the map for the American press, unless we searched for it. Baghdad was at that time a city of over three million, with a thriving economy, a growing acceptance of women in the public sphere, and a flourishing artistic scene. (Iraq is famously a country of poets. Mahmoud Darwish attests to it in his poem "I Remember Al-Sayyâb.") And yet this progress took place under an authoritarian and brutal government. In the complicated history of Iraqi politics there were committed oppositional groups, sometimes affiliated with the government, sometimes underground. Zangana was a member of The Central Leadership Group (an anti-Soviet branch of the Iraqi Communist Party) during a difficult time. It required bravery.

She was also a student of pharmacy at the prestigious Bâb al-Mu'azzam campus of the University of Baghdad. Then there was her arrest and confinement in a series of prisons: Qasr al-Nihaya (for political prisoners, the cruelest of the three), Abu Ghraib (where she spent six months), and Al-Za'afaraniya (a prison for prostitutes, chosen by the government as a way to add insult to imprisonment). Qasr al-Nihaya was once a palace, retrofitted in the Baath period as a prison. (She had visited there, age seven, with her family, as a tourist, not suspecting she would be tortured there fourteen years later.) As for Abu Ghraib, she describes it with understatement as "the normal prison." American readers will recognize the name.

After her release she managed to reenroll at the university, graduated in 1974, and went to Syria, where she worked with Palestinian refugees in the pharmaceutical unit of the Red Crescent (sister institution of the Red Cross)—another selfless commitment, of less interest to biographers. The next step was relocation to England in 1976. Then there are the new developments that residence in England made possible.

She became a successful painter. It was a way, she has said, to distance herself from dark memories. Five years after her arrival, however, the seemingly endless Iran-Iraq war began (it would last eight years). This is the period when conditions in Iraq became progressively worse, and her increasingly public career began.

Eventually oppositional energy among the Iraqi community in England would target the 2002 invasion of Iraq and its aftermath. Earlier the target was Saddam Hussein. (She met her husband Mundher in 1988, at a political rally protesting against the Iraqi government for the murder by chemical weapons of Kurdish civilians.) It was after the invasion that she began to produce the uncompromising body of writing which has made her one of our most prominent observers of the international scene.

Then there is her fiction. The stories of *Packaged Lives* offer us access to a distinctive voice. You often feel that it is grounded in her experience, but there is something else you may become aware of, gradually. You see first a persistent, radical determination to strip away illusion or ideology. Writers always say this is their goal, but Zangana's grasp of experience goes further. She acknowledges the imperfect glimpses we have and exposes not just the event but the surface of memory, with its corrugations, pockmarks, and gaps. You feel in it the authenticity of someone refusing to claim control over what you don't really know.

Her first book to be translated into English, in 1990, leads the reader through details of daily life, childhood memories, and scenes of pain and dread, in hiding or in prison. It is a testimony of humiliation and torture, made more accessible and startling for its emphasis on the way we perceive them. The horrific experience has become a memory. The memory is all you have to work with. The emphasis is even visible in the title: *Through the Vast Halls of Memory* (translating Arabic *Fī arwiqat al-dhākira*), reissued in 2009 under the title *Dreaming of Baghdad*. In the afterword to *Dreaming of Baghdad*, Ferial Ghazoul has described Zangana's style in these terms: "The brutalization of human beings is described in an almost neutral tone but with the minute details of an anatomist." That neutral tone is a remarkable accomplishment. It is memory (fictionalized to avoid betraying friendships), without embellishment or elaboration. She doesn't emphasize how the experience of violence had changed her, how she suffered or how she did or didn't represent the oppositional values of her comrades. It's the memory stripped bare. It is the tone of someone who utterly refuses to portray herself as a victim.

Ghazoul adds that "Zangana's mode of writing liberates the text from the confines of the specific and globalizes the experience." The refusal to embellish memory makes possible a specific, precise focus. Paradoxically, it makes memory more responsible to history. Something circumscribed and contained, an honest portrayal of something near at hand, opens out on bigger issues.

It is not always memory. Sometimes the detail available close at hand is something tangible and small. In "Packaged Life" a goldfinch in a cage is the occasion for a dialogue that explores the nature of freedom. The small thing with the big issue behind it can be a sardonic reality. It may even question the motives of those committed to social change. In

"Packaged Life" a character asks, "Do you think Che Guevara would have become the universal symbol for revolution and an icon for all generations if he had not been handsome?"

Elsewhere the way memory shapes experience amounts to a heroic act of vision. The short story called "Painting" describes the process of staging an art exhibition. The content of the paintings is specific: "He painted them in the aftermath of the US bombings of Iraq, when he was possessed by anger and impotence, so he painted his anger, impotence, love, grief, and fear." We don't see the violence, but in an extraordinary paragraph, we watch a viewer returning to the exhibit, beginning gradually to sense it: "In the days that followed, the painting grew, gradually but steadily, and picked up more shades. It changed . . . The polite quiet statement disappeared. A sigh, almost a scream, shot out of the grays, an open mouth the size of pain." A single painting hanging on a wall, observed closely, contains a comment on history on an enormous, vertiginous scale.

The period around 1990 was rich in oil spills. The spills that have taken precedence in historical memory are the Exxon-Valdez spill off the Alaskan coast (March 1989) and the Mega Borg oil spill in the Gulf of Mexico (July 1990). There was also the Gulf War oil spill of January 1991, at the time of this writing the largest oil spill in history (a discharge of eight million barrels), initiated by Saddam Hussein when his invasion of Kuwait was repelled and his army was in retreat. In a way it was a military tactic, a variant of scorched earth policy, evidently designed to cover their withdrawal. It was also clearly an act of rage.

It would be easy to answer rage with rage. You could place a character on the scene and observe the human misery. The story "Duck" describes the Gulf War oil spill only as it was seen on television, in the West, where the news zeroed in on birds covered with oil rather than the oil itself and its damage to the human world. Birds covered in oil became the icon of the disaster, the photogenic emblem of oil spills, and its effect on characters in London, faced with those oil-covered birds on television, is the focus of the story. It shows the way we learn about the disaster, how an individual experiences history, from a distance. In its way it is funny, in another it is ghastly.

The experience of history can grow out of an amateur's research into archeological texts. There is a character in "Packaged Life" who carries with him two lines of Akkadian, the opening phrases of the creation story referred to as the *Enuma Elish*, which allows a glimpse of the gods who existed before creation (Apsu and Tiamat). L. W. King's translation reads, "When on high the heaven had not been named, / Firm ground below had not been called by name": *enūma eliš lā nabû šamāmū / šapliš ammatu šuma lā zakrat* (James B. Pritchard, *Ancient Near Eastern Texts Relating to the Old Testament*, Princeton Univ. Press, 1950). It is easy to imagine that those lines are at the center of Zangana's vison. In one way they simply express an ideology of ancient Iraq as a model. Zangana does in fact insist on the continuity of ancient Mesopotamia and the current nation of Iraq. The *Enuma Elish*, thought to date back to early in the second millennium BCE, is a good resource to make that argument. But it is not simply an early text. It is also an attempt to visualize existence before creation, that early moment when "neither heaven nor earth had names." A world without names is a world stripped bare, without illusion. It is a formal way to express what a character thinks, more simply, in the short story "Cave": "To be at one with nature is to accept her as she is."

The Iraqi characters of *Packaged Lives* carry the past inside them, invisibly, often a history of disturbing memories that most observers can only guess at. These vignettes allow us to see familiar sights, abroad or at home in London, from the point of view of people who have experienced too much history. They have roots elsewhere, but once we have glimpsed them their experiences are recognizable no matter what background the reader brings to them.

Many years ago, when the first translation of *Through the Vast Halls of Memory* came out, long before I had heard of her, much less met her, I heard Haifa interviewed late at night on Canadian radio. I had no idea who she was, but her clarity and lack of pretense were easy to hear, clear enough that I knew I had to read that book. It was before the days when one could order a book online, but you could place an order by mail from a British bookstore and wait. And, for a long time after the book arrived, there were very few people to discuss it with. One of them was my friend Wen-chin Ouyang. We often discussed what made Haifa's writing extraordinary—her distinctive ability to control a narrative, to weave vignettes, to take incendiary political issues and translate them into human terms. "You know," she added, "she's written a lot more since then." I learned that she and Haifa were friends. And so it came about that Haifa was no longer just a voice on the radio.

And now Wen-chin is the architect and carpenter of this collection, editor and translator, drawing on a deep affinity with the author to make this translation available to us in English. The two share an openness to dialogue and commitment to a straightforward style, without ornament or pretense. *Packaged Lives* is an introduction to a world they know well. Its existence is a testament of friendship.

Dedication

Wen-chin Ouyang

I have known Haifa and Mundher for as long as I have been in London. Lun-Yun joined us much later and not very frequently. Coordinating our globetrotting schedules was never easy. Haifa, Mundher, and I live in London at different intervals dependent on our work routines and life habits. Lun-Yun had his life in Taiwan and visited when he was off and I was still working. We met perhaps no more than twice as a foursome, once at Haifa and Mundher's for dinner and another at a Kurdish-Turkish restaurant for a lunch of kebab on Grand Parade near where I live in the Harringay Ladder. I do not remember what we talked about, but I can still feel Lun-Yun's quiet happiness when we were together. He liked people and got on famously with everyone, especially after a few drinks. Like one of the male protagonists in "Packaged Life," he hugged strangers in pubs, restaurants, trains, taxis, and even streets, and called them brothers when he was tipsy. But he was fastidious about his choice of friends. "The Iraqi couple I met in London," he said to me once, and I cannot remember when, where, or why, "They are good friends." I could always tell when he found kindred spirits, and Haifa and Mundher are kindred spirits. He would have loved the spontaneity of how we came to this project. He would have liked the stories Mundher and I selected.

It was one of those rare beautiful sunny London summer days almost ten years ago when Haifa, Mundher, and I met for lunch on Grand Parade. We exchanged news, gossiped about politics and political leaders, talked about our life and work, and thought about friendships and relationships. I noticed that Haifa had called Mundher a girlfriend in a dedication. "He is like a girlfriend," Haifa exclaimed, "I could tell him everything." Mundher has, of course, read everything Haifa has written. We talked about his favorites and less favorites and one thing led to another and before I knew it, I was suggesting that he make a selection of the short stories he liked the best for me to add my own and I would translate them into English. "But you always say you don't translate," Haifa said in surprise. "I would do it for friends," I answered. Lun-Yun would have done anything for friends. He was not a girlfriend and I did not tell him everything. I did not have to because he felt, knew, and understood. After all we have been friends since 1982. This volume, made up of ten stories Mundher selected and a novella I chose, is about friendship, about its centrality in our life, in our relationship with partners, family, and community. It is also about the itincrant life we live today, and how we manage the diversity of our experiences and the multiplicity of our belongings. Above all, it is about the fundamental humanity in all of us, that even as we cling to our mundane life, with all its trappings, we always find in moments of unexpected epiphany ways to transcend it.

We are Sinbads, the four of us, in our different ways. Wanderlust is our middle name. And none of use lives in our birthplace. Haifa is of Kurdish origin but lived in Baghdad before she moved to London through Damascus and Beirut. Mundher grew up in Baghdad, studied in Moscow, and moved to London, like Haifa, after brief stays in Damascus and Beirut. They now divide their time between London and Tunis. Lun-Yun was born in Dongyin, one of the Matsu islands off the coast of Taiwan, and moved to Taipei when he was fifteen. He went on to study in New York at Manhattan School of Music and Juilliard. He lived in Taipei but taught at a university in Tainan, the old capital of Taiwan. Concerts took him everywhere around the world. And he went on packaged tours with his family, friends, and colleagues. I was born in Taiwan but raised in Libya, where I lived for eighteen years. I did my graduate studies in New York at Columbia University and taught at the University of Virginia, altogether for fifteen years, before I moved to London. I traveled around Europe with my parents, the United States with friends, and Asia and Europe with Lun-Yun. Needless to say, conferences took me to even more places around the world. We divided our time between London and Taipei.

But we always come home no matter how far we wandered, not to a place, but to our family and friends. We more particularly carry our family with us everywhere we go. Haifa in London and Lun-Yun in Taipei still live among their siblings. Haifa sees her brothers frequently and is in touch with them every day, and Lun-Yun and I live in a family complex in Taipei. Mundher and I have more of a virtual relationship with our families, but we are similarly very close to them. Relationships are hard work, and closeness makes them even more complex. We often find ourselves torn between staying and running away from a love that can feel like prison. *Packaged Lives*, inspired by the title of the novella I chose for the collection, is homage to all of us who struggle to commit to relationships and the type of life they impose on us, and at the same time find personal freedoms so we can recharge and return to try again. Life comes in a package, but occasional journeys away from home can provide personal respite. The stories in this volume have in common the theme of the simultaneous need for relationships that anchor who we are and the impulse to run away from them toward what we imagine to be freedom. But the act of running away never takes one to freedom; rather, it reveals even more of the prison houses we live in. There is always that imaginary homeland originating from either our memories of the past or our dreams for the future.

All the protagonists in Haifa's stories, here and elsewhere, are politically engaged Iraqis in exile. They have all found an alternative life, successful or not, outside Iraq, in this case in Britain. But Iraq resides in them, as if they have never left. Their bodies are in London but their hearts and minds stayed behind in Baghdad. The raving mad protagonists of "Evensong," "Chatter," and "Delirium" remained chained to Iraq and her political problems, unable to move on even in their new, comfortable life. The commitment to an imaginary homeland grounded in the past comes to a head with the fantasy for an alternative future in "Duck." Both the past and the future are prisons. How can we escape and be free when even our very bodies are also prisons, as we see in "Refuge" and "Turnstile"? All is not lost, for transcendence is possible. Haifa is at her best when she writes about the fleeting moments of epiphany, in "Cave," "Pilgrimage," "Painting," and "Packaged Life." Poetry, art, history, nature, and occasionally a few stiff drinks can get us there. More often than not these come in one package. Intoxication is a way to describe the loosening of inhibitions, emotional, intellectual, and social, to describe total immersion in contemplation, and of reaching a state when and where borders dissolve. The body becomes one with nature in "Cave," daughter and father, audience and performer, and reality and fantasy merge in "Pilgrimage," mother and son, past and present, reality and imagination fuse in "Painting," and history and dreams for a better future, and Christianity and Islam, come together to provide personal relief and glimpses of nirvana in "Packaged Life."

This is Lun-Yun's private world. He was not religious but he believed in music, art, literature, lessons of the past, and the unity of human experience of what may be called divine regardless of religious denomination. Like Hassoun the goldfinch in "Packaged Life," he played music to lift the spirits. He collected paintings of nature and music that offered contemplations on what is beyond reach of our senses. He read books about the past. History was always on his mind. He loved parables. He sat quietly in churches and temples for long hours. He had a particular fondness for Buddhist temples we discovered in the mountains. We inevitably went to a Zen temple when we were in Japan. We walked to the Tibetan temple almost every day when he taught at the InterHarmony Summer Music Festival in Arcidosso, Tuscany. He visited the Dharma Drum Mountain Monastery often and signed up for a three-day Chan retreat once in Taiwan. He would have loved Haifa's mountains as well as her stories.

Mountains, whether in "Cave" or "Packaged Life," are sites of epiphany. The climb taxes the body and exercises patience but the reward is priceless.

Sitting alone with the clouds up there on a mountaintop, looking quietly at heavens above one's head,
or beholding the earth reaching the far end of the
horizon below one's feet, soothes the mind, calms
the heart, and revives the body. The ruins of human
civilization and relics of the past in the background
deliver a stark contrast for contemplation. There is
nothing more cleansing of the soul than the stories
of human triumph over the darkness of their history
and the violence of their nature, whether by simply surviving atrocities and overcoming their worst
impulses or, against the odds, by reaching out to
others, to help them survive and thrive. The pilgrimage to St. Patrick's Grave would be, I am sure, Lun-
Yun's favorite.

The stories Haifa tells seem like parables. Her
simple language is deceptive. Keen, subtle, humor-
ous, her translucent narrative observes, questions,
and moves characters and events but never judges,
instructs, or preaches. She leaves you alone to experience the world and characters she lovingly creates, at
your own pace and without interference. As a friend,
she is like that. So are Mundher and Lun-Yun. They
have given me homes but have never made demands. I
am always free to come and go. The stories have been
sitting in a drawer in our Taipei home for almost ten
years now. I began working on them in January, four
months after Lun-Yun passed away. Translation, like
Haifa and Mundher's friendship, kept me grounded
and focused. Above all, the stories took me to new

parts of the world, places I had never been, and at the same time brought me back to a familiar home, to the world Lun-Yun and I shared. For this, and for their friendship, I am most grateful.

Packaged Lives

From *The House of Ants* (1996)

1

Evensong

One

He felt it was extremely necessary to write a short introduction to explain the story he had begun to write four months ago. He has not finished yet. He had decided against it a few days ago, but this morning as he woke to the sound of loud raindrops on the skylight of his room the idea came back to him in full force. The introduction would be absolutely essential, he thought, for he would want to explain the recurrence of two elements in his stories and for that matter all his writings: diary and dream. He had been writing diaries since childhood, and dreams haunt his body at an average of two per night. He would have cared more in his youth to explain these, but he has changed. Change did not happen to him suddenly. On the contrary, it came to him slowly, sauntering in his footsteps with the passage of time, accompanying him every step of the way as he grew older and

From *The House of Ants* (1996), 67–73.

consumed more Arak, whiskey, a shot and a beer day and night.

The straw that broke the back of his self-confidence and of his ability to formulate ideas and sentences was the title a young critic chose for her article on his stories. It had come as a slap on his face in the morning. He usually opened his letters and the magazines he received regularly in proportion to his contributions. The title was "Hackneyed Stories by a Writer Innovation Left Behind." What was she trying to prove in her article? Why was innovation demanded only of him and no one else? Everything new he contributed was not enough? Was his name not always linked to the leadership of innovation? What was innovation in a world that recycled its fashions every twenty years? A world that reprocessed ideas for feature articles and regular columns in newspapers and magazines. Ideas, the so-called new ideas, that came from the distant Middle Ages, a time when kings clung desperately to their thrones until their subjects breathed their last.

What did she want from him? Why would she censure him for turning to his diaries? Did they not represent his genuine voice, and a full record of what was happening around him, not just the ups and downs? What was wrong with his dreams? Were they not his only moments of epiphany, when he stepped out of his masquerade, took off his masks, stopped hiding behind other people's voices, faces, gestures, and all kinds of languages not his own?

Two

He took a sip from his fourth whiskey and lifted the glass up toward the ceiling lamp, twirling the remaining cube of ice at the bottom, before he drained the last drops. He wanted to push all the papers piled up on his desk away from him, to scatter them page by page onto the floor of his room, to kick at his books, and to tear up his diaries into bits so small he would never be able to put them back again, even if he had wanted, as he habitually did, to reread them every morning as soon as he woke up. He wanted to stand on his desk and scream at all the criticism and the whole wide world, these are my stories, this is who I am, stressing every word, as if he did not want to spit it out of his body on its own but accompanied by his soul and the validity of his dreams, in all their plenitude, dreams he had embraced and believed in his youth but had not affected him in any way or mattered to him very much recently. He did not move an inch though. He sat there on his chair, staring at his notebook, papers, his glass of whiskey, and the first line of the introduction to his stories. He muttered between his tightly pursed lips, almost violently, this is who I am.

Three

The only important decision he had to make was whether he should get up and refill his glass with more whiskey or stop drinking. He hesitated for a brief moment and decided in favor of whiskey. He definitely needed another drink before he could write the introduction to the story, before the words would flow under his pen as effortlessly as they used to. He lifted his whiskey glass again and looked at the bright light of the lamp coming through two layers of thick glass. How quiet is my home, he thought, so quiet he could only hear his watch ticking. It is nine o'clock in the evening, no, it is eight-thirty. He set it this way so he could fast-forward the slow evening hours, so he could start drinking earlier and go to bed earlier. Maybe if he could climb up the tall ladder of drink faster to reach inebriation and epiphany he would be able to get his momentous task over with right away. He would finish both the introduction and the story, and at the same time stifle the voice agitating inside for him to write. How he wished he could drag that voice out of his body, fasten his hands around its throat and throttle it to eternal silence. Do they not realize how fatigued he is? Do they not know what homelessness does to one physically and mentally? The taste of the salt of sweat pouring out of bodies no longer able to grasp anything would send anyone into isolation.

Couldn't they picture what happens to a homeless man at night? Dreams attack him when he is at his weakest, not quite awake but not asleep either, tossing and turning, craving moments of oblivion.

Hallucinations concocted by a brain sick with fatigue drown him in a viscous universe out of which he would emerge swamped in liquids discharged by his fearful cells. Innovation? What are they talking about? What kind of innovation do they expect from a man who cannot even see clearly, his mind under the protective shield of alcohol and his vision distracted by the colorful talismans of intoxication. These talismans parade before his eyes, night after night, like supermodels on a catwalk, dizzyingly changing from one designer dress to another. They reclaim him from those who want to take him away and restore him to his mindless daily routines, long hours spent on waiting for the evening to arrive. The evening hours are stretched out in a pool of alcohol, surrounded by a few snacks and some ideas. Heavy, violent, and fermenting ideas stared him in the face, like the first sentence of his introduction to his new story: "He felt it was extremely necessary to write a short introduction to explain his story."

Why does he want to explain his story? Is it not enough that he wrote it? Why did the article pain him to such an extent? How did he let the words of the young critic crawl under his skin? He took pride in his thick skin, did he not, in his ability to push under the rug the havoc real emotions wreaked? He said, laughing aloud, "Let's be realistic, it is either that my skin is tattered or her words have touched a raw wound. I refuse to talk about it."

Four

He was in his late fifties. He could see himself weave
a web of isolation around himself. He was afraid to
walk down streets unfamiliar to him. He avoided
going alone to restaurants, town halls, galleries, and
museums. All eyes were on him, he felt, and no one
else. He was afraid of meeting people he did not know.
Having to answer questions without prior prepa-
ration horrified him. At the end of his first English
class—and it lasted an eternity—he decided to miss
the second lesson, the third, and what might have followed. He would not be able to learn a new language
at fifty. He saw no point in repeating demonstrative
nouns and pronouns after the teacher, like an idiot, or
putting them in useful sentences. He could use some
real exchange of ideas, not English phrases for buying a pound of tomatoes or a bus ticket. How many
years would he spend learning a language, of which
he knew only a few words, before he would be able to
fluently exchange ideas with its speakers?

He searched in vain for the spirit who protected
human beings from boredom and guarded their life-
long desires, passions, and fascinations, which drove
them to seek for the unknown beyond the familiar
horizon. He pressed his lips together tightly. Suddenly he felt the magic of the words he was uttering
very slowly and carefully, the words that were slid-
ing down the edges of his lips: where is surprise? I
will tell her, he said, that I too am bored stiff with

writing diaries and recording dreams. They are close, too close even for me, and I, too, want to write about distant topics, topics that do not have their arrows directed at my heart, about other people, about far-reaching ideas. Three words fell into his glass, hitting the bottom with varying force: events . . . about . . . distant . . . He lifted his glass toward the lamp, this time, to see the words gathering at its base. If only he could rescue the sentence, he thought, he would surely be able to write the introduction to his story and the story, well, at least, his short story.

In total mental and physical excitement, he lost the permanent frown on his forehead and began to watch the words glide from one side of his whiskey glass to another. One drop, one word, another drop, one more word . . . He began to rock himself with a tenderness he showed no one but himself, and only in moments of ecstasy, and to swing himself high in an imaginary seesaw. A drop, a word, another drop, one more word . . . One more glass of whiskey and the words would fill the page. "One more glass of whiskey and I will fill the pages with a new kind of writing, with an innovative text that will excite even my old joy." Another glass.

Very carefully he reached out for the notebook of his dreams. He wanted to write his next dream. He now believed he could invent his dreams, influence them, even create dreams from his thoughts. His dreams were his very life, while he was only one of the elements, all of which have a life of their own in his dreams. Fantastic hallucinations. Could there be anything more fantastic than fabricating dreams? His whole body heavy with drunkenness, he lifted his glass high up toward the lamp in great excitement to drink to the health of his dreams, his whiskey, and the young critic who disturbed a deep wound.

Only alcohol could stop the bleeding inside him. He wanted to have both the here and now and the there and then. If only he could see through the crystal of his glass the mirage of ecstasy, the paradise of souls, and the full-blown sails on a beautiful day. He wanted to break free from the moment, to lose his profound fear, and feel again the flames of the burning spirit of his youth.

The more he looked the less he perceived until he saw nothing.

February 1994

2

Chatter

Place: South of London. A small flat on the ground floor. A big room divided into two. The first half for living and sleeping. A couch is the centerpiece. It is sparsely furnished. A small, low table. A television and a video player with a few videocassettes scattered around them. A wooden floor covered by a Persian carpet. A telephone on the couch next to a notepad and a pen. The second half is a library. Books piled up on shelves reaching up to the ceiling covering two facing walls. More piles of books, newspapers, and newspaper cuttings on the floor. A large wooden desk. A computer, a printer, and books of all kinds—science, philosophy, politics, literature, the visual arts, and exhibition and museum catalogues—occupy the surface. Two doors. One to the kitchen and the other to the narrow hallway leading up to the bathroom and the front door.

Time: Friday, 16 May 1995, 8:30 a.m.

From *The House of Ants* (1996), 165–72.

Player: Adnan. Forty-six. Tall, thin, with an oddly proportioned figure. A rectangular block of chest and stomach with no waist. Calm facial features offset by excitable mannerisms. Dressed in a white shirt and a pair of gray trousers.

He is speaking on the phone to a woman who could be his wife or girlfriend. Her physical presence is of no importance. He is not listening to her. He does not expect her to respond either. He does not see her at all. She is his sounding board. He is simply thinking out loud. This happens every time he talks on the phone.

He drinks a lot of tea and moves nonstop between the kitchen and the bathroom. Quick, successive, chopped-up sentences. He is afraid of losing track of them, and of his ideas. He eats while talking. He writes while talking. His favorite place is his chair facing the window looking over the street behind his desk.

Isn't it strange that human beings have been thinking obsessively about the same issue for thousands of years! I mean, the relationship between man and woman, like what the television series presented last night, I mean *The Politician's Wife*. We were affected by the wife's position. Many things go into the making of a character. Complex factors. It's not really like what we think. There's religion, the oath of fidelity, the social contract, a sense of betrayal . . . There's morality and dishonesty . . . There's deception . . .

There're other complicated factors, like the father-son or mother-daughter relationships, but these don't seem to take up the same amount of our attention. What do you think?

He gets up from his chair, goes to the kitchen, and returns with a piece of old cheese on a small plate. He wipes the mold off the cheese and cuts it into thin slices. He brings another plate of sliced tomato, cucumber, and brown bread. He mutters.

The skin of the cucumber is thicker than the cucumber itself. It feels like the buildup of chemical compounds and wax.

He looks at the calendar. The picture displayed is of a painting by an impressionist artist.

Speaking of relationships, take this painting, for example, it's both strange and attractive. Two young girls. Sisters. One has a strong personality. She's the domineering one. The other plays the role of the mother. She looks after her sister with tenderness. She brushes her hair. The features of the strong sister remind me of Scarlett O'Hara, the heroine of *Gone with the Wind*.

He eats quickly. He puts a morsel in his mouth with one hand and with the other brings up another morsel close to his lips. As if he were in an eating competition. For each morsel he piles a slice of cheese, a slice of tomato, and a slice of cucumber on a slice of bread. He presses these together tightly with his fingers in case any should fall to the ground on the way to his mouth.

I'm worried. I didn't feel comfortable with Peter yesterday. The problem with Peter is that he thinks he has a monopoly over language. I gave him a report on our project and till now he's read only a few pages. He nodded his head and said it was good, very good, but this would mean changing his project. He meant of course changing the terms used and their meanings. He has wonderful ideas but he can't express them clearly. All I did in my report was to present a clear and brief overview. For him though there are other things to consider. First of all, there's the question of age and at what age a person becomes resistant to change, and secondly, how fast can one change . . . I notice that he pauses sometimes when we're talking and says, stop, stop, I can't follow you, my working memory is not functioning anymore . . . For Peter thinking is a process; it is like a computer, if you give it too much information it can't process it. Or it gets confused.

Knowledge is a process and it must be given time, according to Peter. He pauses, looks away, and thinks, and he can take days or weeks to think. At our meeting with the head of the department yesterday, he kept saying, "Give me credit for my experience." I was annoyed. I am still annoyed. Some people stand in the way of progress because they don't know how to communicate. We're now facing a problem that may delay our project. Whenever I suggested a question or proposed an answer or came up with a theoretical explanation, he always gave the same response, wait until we have the results of the experiment, until we have analyzed these results, and have looked at the final picture. Only then can we know the answer. My position is completely different. What I'm saying is that waiting for results shouldn't prevent us from looking for answers or talking about them. He said we must learn to live with our uncertainties. Why? Don't we have the experience, knowledge, and experiments we have made to help us overcome the uncertainties? Why do we postpone looking for answers? Fine. He's not a bad human being, Peter, and he may be right about this. But I'm like Abbas-Can't-Wait. Does Peter know the story of Abbas-Can't-Wait? They have something similar in English proverbs, like Peeping Tom, but I don't really know the similarities. Speaking of proverbs and words . . .

He goes to the kitchen, returns with a cup of tea, and stands in front of the window absentmindedly.

I was thinking of triliteral verbs in Arabic and how to conjugate them. I know we have to strip every word down to a triliteral root, but how do you get to those three letters? I read, I can't remember where, that triliteral verbs come from putting two biliteral verbs together. The word H-J-R, "stone," for example, is made up from H-J, "pilgrimage," plus J-R, "to trail," like "to train around the black stone during the pilgrimage to Mecca." And the word KH-T-R, "danger," is made up of KH-T, "to write, to draw a line," plus, uh, T-R, but wait—there isn't any T-R.

He repeats in monotony.

KH-T, to write, KH-T, to draw a line.

What matters to me is the straight line, or what connects two points in a straight line. Its relationship with geometry interests me. I discussed geometry with Peter and Robert yesterday. They say geometry is no longer important. It's an outdated science. I think they're wrong. I have my own theory. Geometry, the science of point, line, and flat surface, can be applied to other sciences. Geometry can help explain other sciences. Take the example of a child looking at a certain point in front of him. He draws a hypothetical line, though unknowingly, between his eye and the point. When he moves his eye in another direction, whichever direction that may be, he does nothing but draw straight lines linking the eye and what it sees.

He adopts the mannerism of a teacher giving a lesson.

This is from the perspective of the child. What about the person watching him? When he looks at the child looking at something from his position he draws a triangle that connects three points. While he looks at the child drawing a straight line, he is also looking at the straight line. We have here a flat surface.

He reaches out for the phone and dials a number.

Hussein, good morning, I'm very busy now, call you in five minutes.

He returns the handset to the base and leaves for the bathroom. He returns, still talking.

I must call Faiza. I will cancel my appointment with her. I don't feel comfortable with this woman.

Too ambitious. Too pushy in too many ways. Now, right, what about the root of triliteral verbs? If the theory of merging two biliteral verbs is correct . . . This reminds me of the Chinese language, which is pictorial. If we want to say "stable" we draw a house and an animal, and if we want to say "farm" we draw a house and a plant. It has remained a pictorial language to this day. If we go back to the origin of any language, Arabic, for example, what stops a language from resembling the early human utterances? A child begins with making sounds like these.

He makes childish noises, moving his hands and feet.

Ga, Ka, and Ta, no, no, no, these come later. He begins with Ma, Ba, and Da, or, or Baba, Dada. Ma is the mother, Ba is the father, Da is for siblings and pointing, and maybe Sa is for sky and Tha for earth. A letter pronounced in a particular way may not be proof enough for the beginning of things. Two letters add more force.

He tries calling Hussein again. He waits. He takes the phone and sits behind his desk.

Good morning again. How are you? It pained me to read Dr Naaman's article. I have thought about it and formulated the following position. Yes, political and economic adequacies aside, we also need technology and pragmatic strategies for coexistence. It's almost the same as the Opposition. Do you support it?

He speaks in a sharp tone and spits out words in great excitement.

If you're truly democratic you have to work with the people, not the businessmen. There're such things as history, public opinion, and the street. The street may be emotional and reckless but you still have to respect it. It's the role of the intellectuals and thinkers to serve the strategies put forward by the nation and the people. We don't have the constitutional structure or legal mechanism to represent the nation . . .

Silence

Everything is going in one direction and this is wrong. We must write and analyze to make things clear.

Longer silence

Not exploring an idea fully is dangerous. Nobody is challenging the might of America and Israel and this is dangerous. We have to look at other axes of power. What's China's position? For example, what will happen if she decides to play a role in the future? This is a different axis. Is there an alternative to American domination and whatever Israel dictates?

Silence

No . . . Understood . . . Yes . . . I know . . . Clarity can be dangerous . . . This makes us trash the views of the people . . .

Silence

Some people say that America is capable of anything and everything. In my opinion, we have to point out the contradictions within America itself. I mean we have to come up with proposals that go against the taken-for-granted position of compliance.

He calms down a bit. His tone softens.

The pragmatic position is what I said, to focus on the present and go in the direction I asked you to take. What do I want? When you write or give a lecture, take into account other perspectives.

Silence

True . . . Yes . . . This saves the cause. Democracy is even more indispensable when we are under siege . . . Your article was pretty good. The position it suggests is like the one taken by the ancien régime. The people respect it because it is better than complete submission.

Silence

I know . . . I have a very small suggestion though. I would begin with the wider context and change the way you address your readers.

Silence

You speak to people from the perspective of the theories that proclaim the end of history, the end of ideologies, and the rise of a new world system. This is where you and I don't always see eye to eye.

He interrupts the person on the other end of the phone sharply.

I know you don't say that explicitly, I know, but there is a link between what you write and those theories. Your current position is based on this approach even if you're not fully aware of it.

Silence

Yes, balance, accumulation and balance, two ideas, this is a political philosophy . . .

Silence

The nation needs multiple perspectives . . .

Silence

The story . . .

Silence

First of all, can we deal intelligently with the American position on the Middle East? Secondly, will it be possible to propose a collaborative project that will unite all the Arab nations?

Silence. Then he interrupts the person on the other end of the phone sharply again.

No, I'm not being emotional. This is a fundamental question, and you must raise your writings to a higher standard so that they can have a bigger impact.

He laughs.

I know . . . Multiply your perspectives and you'll have a bigger audience . . . No, no . . . I have . . . This is wrong . . . It's clear who is patriotic . . . I know . . . The phone can sometimes help make ideas clear . . . I know . . . The people are fed up inside . . . Siege everywhere . . . The size of our tragedy is so big people just want a solution to our problem, any solution, and to start again, like Africa, who are now inviting the colonizers to return . . . OK . . . See you soon . . .

He puts the phone back in its place. He remains standing. He looks out at the street. Quiet inside and outside except for the ticking of the clock. He looks up at the wall clock. It is a quarter to ten. He jumps.

Damn, I have a meeting at the university at ten-thirty.

He rushes out of the room, puts on his coat, comes back to retrieve a big envelope, and goes out again. We hear the loud slam of the door.

February 1996

3

Delirium

In his late forties, he has the look of familiarity that anyone who meets him thinks he knows him. Short, with a head of thick black hair touched by white at the temple. Dressed in a white shirt with blue stripes and a pair of gray trousers.

He is waving his hands and reaches out with his right hand to massage his moustache, forgetting that he had shaved it off when he first arrived in London. His slightly bulging eyes are sparkling with keen intelligence. His emotions are clear for everyone to see, in his trembling lips and the foam gathering at the two corners of his mouth.

He lives in a small room designed for a single person. A pink spread covers the small bed. Pink curtains drape over the window. A small table and two chairs stand by the bed. A pile of books is under the table, and another pile next to the bed on a small pink rug. To the right of the room is what looks like

From *The House of Ants* (1996), 129–32.

a kitchen counter. It is equipped with an electric hub and a sink sandwiched between a cupboard above for cups and plates and another below for pots and pans. Next to it, in a corner, is a small fridge with an electric kettle sitting on top.

Night falls. The light emitted by the only lamp in the room is too bright for the suffocating size of the room. The man never stops moving. He sits on the edge of the bed for a few minutes and gets up. He goes to the kitchenette to prepare a cup of tea, then forgets what he is doing. He sits on the chair, stares at the blank pages, and gets up again. He opens the fridge door. He looks inside absentmindedly. He slams the door shut again. Or he leaves it slightly ajar.

All the while he raves.

I swear by God I'll spend the rest of my life exposing their corruption. Thirty years of my life I've wasted in their service. Class struggle, free homeland, and the people's right to pursue happiness, these were all illusions. All the while we, the young and naive, did the work. We mobilized people, increased party membership, distributed pamphlets, and ran from place to place. We abandoned our families and children. The married men left their wives and the unmarried their fathers, mothers, and young brothers and sisters. Every single one of us paid with his youth and life and for what, to be victims of both the regime and the party. How many of us? Ha! And your highness tells me to forget the past, turn over a new leaf, and start life anew! After all this and you want me to swear by the grave of my father whose funeral I managed to miss, why, because I was too busy serving the party? Don't argue. Execute then argue. I saw everything but never argued. I left the house at dawn and got back only after midnight. All that time I told myself they would reward me one day, and I would be like them, living the good life. It's true that the life of struggle was difficult and had to be lived in secret, but between you and me it wasn't always difficult or secretive for everyone. I mean there are people and there are people. Party leadership traveled and had a good life pretty much all the time outside the country. They took their children, relatives, and lovers with them, to study, to seek medical treatment, you name it. All membership vacancies were reserved, and when we asked for whom, someone would answer, "reserved is reserved, Comrade," or "all vacancies are filled this year, Comrade, maybe next year, don't forget, Comrade, your existence inside is very necessary, among the people, among the nation." If only it were my father's revolution and my grandfather's Marxism!

So I stay close to the nation and the people, but what about you, and the leadership or the members of the central committee? Where is their place? In Moscow, Bulgaria, Hungary, to be even closer to the people and the nation? How many times did I apply for membership? Ten? Twenty? Every time they had an excuse. Let me tell you one more time, they all are, all of them, corrupt!

What? Are you telling me Ahmed is not like them? Are you calling me a liar? That I have something to gain from telling you what I'm telling you now? What gain? For your information, I have a BA from the Faculty of Management and Economics, and if it's about envy and jealousy like you say, I could have stayed in my job and got myself cozy with the Ba'thist regime. A lot of good would have come out of it for me, instead of this tiny prison cell in a country that rarely sees the sun. Do you think I enjoy watching the Arabs rush from one palace to another or one presidential office to another? Ahmed? Of course I know him. I've known him since he was in the student union. He was our neighbor too. You think you know Ahmed better than I do! Of course he didn't want membership in the party. Do you know why he declined party membership? Why did he refuse to go to Moscow, do you reckon? Because he was happy in Syria! Everything he wanted he found in Syria. Why would he trouble himself, go to a foreign country, learn a new language, and board in a military school? Syria was better for him. He fought his battles at meetings in the afternoon and drank blissfully at night. The best life! Food and drink at the expense of the people. I know Ahmed very well. He is the laziest man in the country! If you left him under a palm tree he would sit there until a date fell into his mouth. He would never get himself worked up about anything. Entre nous, Ahmed was the poorest member of the political office but, like all of them, he put his personal interest above everything else—he would have left the party if he hadn't gotten paid his money, not like me, stuck with the nobodies in the middle of nowhere.

And, why don't you talk about Fawzi, yes, *Abu al-Qurun*, Comrade Fawzi, the father of horns, the pimp, please, don't laugh, I gave him that nickname ages ago. What do you hear about him these days? He's a big investor now. Let me ask you, it's my turn to ask questions, where do you think he got the funds to start with? Donations made by the poor people to the party for hardworking laborers, the money I, and others, collected for the party year in and year out, for how many years now, how many? It went straight into the belly of the big brother, the biggest investor, the father of all commercial and cultural projects. He now owns a cultural center and a publishing house. He curries favors with writers and poets and sells even the stories of the people living lucklessly in exile. The worst is that he sells morality in our name and at our expense. Remember when Comrade Siham made a complaint, remember, let's not talk about it, it's better! You now know why I'm so edgy, why I feel angry all the time, like my body is poisoned from top to bottom? Look at it, look at my body! Do you need a second example? I'll give you a third, a fourth, a tenth, any given number matching the few strands of hair on your head. I have evidence for every word I say. Do you need another example? Let me think, ha, yes, remember that big shot historian, the luminary of the scholarly community with one foot in the grave? It turned out that he was on the list of names who were receiving a salary from the KGB. And that famous artist, so very innovative, so creative, who taught everyone the meaning of magic? He now lives in great luxury in Paris. He was a small spy whose only ambition was to become a big spy. Spy for whom, you ask? Let me tell you, for anyone who would pay. Look, my dear, it's not about who pays but about who pays more. You want me to shut up? *Allahu Akbar*! We're in the blessed month of Ramadan and I'm fasting! I swear by God Almighty I will spend the rest of my life exposing their corruption, wherever I go, at every meeting and symposium, I will go and expose them. Why do I waste my time? No, no, this is not a waste of my time; it's my duty, my investment, a huge investment in the future, so that others will not be deceived as I had been. Look here, look at me, living in a room not even good enough for dogs, while every one of them lives in a grand palace.

Do you know what they're doing now besides their investments, commercial ventures, and espionage? Believe it or not, let me tell you, they have become democratic; they're all for democracy, just like what the proverb says: "It's the same donkey with a different saddle." Not only that, they have all joined the Opposition too. Imagine. In a flicker of the eye, they took the rags of proletariat dictatorship off their bodies and put on them the silk robes of democracy. Of course, of course, it's for the better. Without a doubt America is mightier now. America pays in dollars, and of course they all get their salaries in dollars, in hard currency. Democracy these days is the market with the highest return. It looks cleaner and more beautiful too, without the ogre of Communism, the scythe, the hammer, or the workers. Damn Communism, Marxism, and Socialism.

Only a few days ago they organized a conference under a new name. I met one of them, who argued with me so pompously you would think he'd been democratic all his life. His father was democratic, his mother was democratic, he went on and on, "why not, we'll learn, the entire nation must learn, democracy is new to us and we must help people to understand it." To no avail. "The chicken came back the same way it left." We're back to educating the people and nation and helping them, as if it wasn't enough what they did to them. They abandoned Communist organizations, class struggle, and the rights of workers and farmers for democracy. As if it wasn't enough! Before we knew it, it was our fault, the fault of those who served them for years, and the fault of the people and the nation. One of them got up on stage and proclaimed from the podium: "The history of our nation is full of cruelty and violence. We need years to be able to learn democracy."

Son of a bitch, what is democracy and what is educating the nation? Who is qualified to educate the nation, you, or you, you who've never known the nation? If only America, America, if only . . . You still imagine you can deceive the nation?

You think if you organize a symposium or a conference in London with one of you cheering and another
disparaging, we want democracy, the people are not
ready, you think this will help you? I will never give
up on my responsibility. I will expose them wherever
they are, these sick people, even if it kills me.

March 1995

From *Beyond Our Horizon* (1997)

4

Duck

For Ibtisam al-Khalifa

"Why did you break up?"

He was tired. He had just finished a forty-eight-hour shift at the hospital. Still, he welcomed his friend Tony's invitation to have a pint before heading home. As soon as he accepted, he began bracing himself for questions about his personal life and about the reasons he and Suad split up. He did feel he had to meet Tony. For one thing, he is their common friend, and for another they both owe him a great deal. Tony, who is a doctor himself, has chosen to work in a clinic in the neighborhood where he lives, to be close to his patients and away from the bureaucracy of hospital administration, "the kind of bureaucracy Suad navigates so well," as he often said jokingly.

From *Beyond Our Horizon* (1997), 99–113.

This translation originally appeared as "The Duck That Broke the Mule's Back," *Middle Eastern Literatures* 21 (2–3): 244–50. Reprinted by permission of Taylor & Francis Ltd., http://www.tandfonline.com.

Adnan took a big sip of beer and swallowed deeply. He stretched his legs to relax even more, and to shake off fatigue and tension. They were sitting at a small table near a window overlooking the hospital. Like an Iraqi policeman. When he takes a day off, he spends it at a café across the street from the police station.

"I called Suad a couple of days ago. I asked her why did you break up? She told me what she has been doing and thinking about. She didn't talk about her work as she usually did, about her disagreements with the hospital administration, or about her daily conflicts with her specialist colleagues, strangely enough. Instead she talked at length about a schedule packed with gatherings and meetings. I said I must be mistaken, am I really talking to Suad? She laughed and said yes, political gatherings and meetings. I said with whom? She said humanitarian organizations, and organizations for the defense of the environment and protection of animals, and I recently took part in a conference on the defense of human rights. I said, these meetings, are they attended by Iraqis? She said of course, Tony, you may not believe it but I have changed so much."

Adnan listened to Suad's news calmly, with the relief of someone who has had a heavy weight lifted from his chest. He was looking across the street at the hospital, at the twelve-story building. He was seeing himself dragging his body across the corridors in exhaustion. Should he tell Tony about the last time he saw Suad? At a symposium on the defense of human rights, where he introduced her as "an Iraqi woman suffering from the pains of exile." He gazed at Tony's features, his pale skin and thin hair. He was exhausted like him, like all doctors, whose worlds are crowded with patients. "One thing this city does so well is that it metes out unending exhaustion on its citizens."

"Why did you break up?"

"To be perfectly honest, I don't know, maybe because our personalities are so different," he looked at Tony affectionately, "or maybe because she has truly changed while I stayed the same, or maybe it's the duck," he laughed out aloud, "the duck that broke the mule's back."

Suad

Until that moment she did not know very much about ducks. Ducks were birds of both the land and the water. They swam and walked on land. They were birds of the land and the air. They walked and flew. She had her own descriptions for ducks. She saw them in public gardens in London, and in Shatt al-Washwash Creek in Baghdad. She saw them as fat women wobbling down the street, hilariously shaking their large buttocks, the bobbing and quivering layers of fat inflating even more their puffed-up plumage. But the difference between London ducks and Shatt al-Washwash ducks is huge. London ducks command respect. Children and the elderly feed them with affection. They look lovingly at the ducks eating breadcrumbs they throw at them. Japanese tourists compete to take photos of them. Shatt al-Washwash ducks were on the other hand pitiful. They were dirty, just like the children gathering around them on the banks of the creek, and were afraid to leave the water because they knew what fate was waiting for them. A crowd of children ran after them, threw stones at them, and would try, if they caught them, to pluck out their feathers.

Suad never cared very much about the ducks, not those living in the Royal St. James Park, or those living in the putrid waters of Shatt al-Washwash Creek. Not until she saw a duck blackened by oil from the spill on the British TV screen.

Shatt al-Washwash

What distinguishes Shatt al-Washwash, a small town located to the west of Baghdad, is its creek. The city was at one point famous for fruit orchards and clover fields. That was before it was invaded by government projects for residential homes and shopping centers, and by the five-year plan to pave the only street in the city. In the summer, when the temperature rose above what the government had announced, an odor wafting from the creek would attack the nostrils of the citizens, sticking to their nose hair so unrelentingly that they could never get rid of it or even forget it. It was futile for women to close the doors and windows, or turn on the desk and ceiling fans, for the stink from the creek would form a thick fog that hovered above the city and engulfed the streets and houses.

The creek water was not exactly putrid, but it ran slowly, and people who lived on the two banks used it as their rubbish bin. Life existed side by side with death, living beings with castaways. Ducks, mallard, eels, predatory fish, frogs, worms, bristle worms, rotten leftover vegetables, rusty empty cans, slippers and shoes, bottles, broken glass, and even feminine napkins. Against all expectations, the creek, or the little stream as the citizens of the city called it when they despised it the most, never got landfilled as everyone demanded. On the contrary, it acquired a new role after the 14th of July Revolution, in the year 1958 to be precise, that scrapped the idea completely. The hateful creek became the natural checkpoint separating the original people of Shatt al-Washwash living on the right bank from the people of al-Sarayif living on the left. The transformation did not take place over night. Rather, it took a long time, relatively speaking, starting with the arrival of the Abu Kazim family, immigrating here from the city of al-'Imara in the south of Iraq. They built their first mud house on the left bank, and from there they built an entire Sarayif shantytown, then a bridge connecting the two banks.

Suad

Why did we move to Shatt al-Washwash? I asked my mother about our old house but I can't remember her answer. She said I didn't listen. Suddenly we found ourselves in a new house where foul air filled our noses. I used to cover my nose with my hand or handkerchief, but I soon gave up the habit and the smell became a part of my life. How I hated Shatt al-Washwash. I can't decide why. Was it because I saw disgusting barefoot children diving into the creek either to swim, or cross the creek, or chase after the ducks, only to come out and stink up the air even more? Or because my mother told me not to play with them? Or was it because they strutted before me when I wouldn't play with them? Or because they grew rougher and more aggressive the more they failed to make me join them? Or was it because of the severed human leg I saw floating in the creek when I was standing on its bank? How old was I? Nine?

The policemen came and fished out of the green water one limb after another until they recovered the whole body except for the head. From that day I never went near the creek again. It became forbidden to children. "Suad, come home straight from school, don't play in the street, it's all dusty, dirty, and full of Sarayif kids." Kids played on the dirt roads, while I sat at the threshold of our front door with a copy of Egyptian comics, *Samir*, in my hands. The oldest of the kids threw a stone at me. I looked at him, at his white *dishdasha* robe, at his bare feet, in total revulsion. He came near me and I put my hand on my nose to insult him even more. With a sudden move, he lifted his *dishdasha* and pointed at his member, then ran off with his gang. I ran away in horror, into the house, never to sit at the front door again.

When I was a teenager I kept my own company. I had no friends. I used to ask myself, I who always studied hard to be at the top of my class, "Do I have to spend the rest of my life here? Escaping from one book into another, walking in the streets of a city where I dare not look up so as to not see what I won't like, living in a rotten, dusty city that got attacked by flies during the day and mosquitoes at night, with half of its inhabitants ill with trachoma and the other half with Bilharzia, tape worms, and tuberculosis?"

Adnan

I look at her now and see the woman I was meeting for the first time at my cousin's wedding. She kept her distance from the party and looked on as if she was watching kids play. She got my attention right away. Tall, her fair skin untouched by Baghdad's hot sun or air, and her hair cut short unlike other women I knew. She stood there, proud and aloof, as if she wanted to keep away from the others. I asked my sister about her, and she gave me a full report. "She is a pharmacist and her name is Suad. You might know her father, Hajji Hakim? Do you remember him? Her dream is to complete her studies abroad and live outside the country." I had already secured a scholarship to study in London and said to my sister jokingly, "If she marries me, all her dreams will come true."

I look at her and feel my love for her. It has not changed. I was a young doctor dreaming of changing the world, at least changing some things I couldn't really put my finger on yet. Changing Suad seemed as if it would be easy. Her coldness toward my Iraqi friends and their families did not bother me. I said to myself her nature was different, she was busy with her studies, and I came up with excuses for her when a friend visited and she withdrew, very politely, from our living room. When she stopped writing letters and calling her family in Iraq I thought it was temporary and she would soon miss them and get back in touch. She would learn to see the homeland from afar and rediscover every bit of it lovingly and affectionately. Like all my dreams I have watched crumble, Suad did not change. She did extremely well in her studies and very quickly she became a specialist in a prestigious hospital. She came out of her isolation, learned how to drive and swim, joined an expensive sports club, and made new friends who called and asked for Sally when I answered the phone. She had her own friends outside my Iraqi circle, and she continued to withdraw into herself like a tightly wound rope whenever my friends visited. For her sake, or for the sake of avoiding her haughty looks and quarrels, I stopped inviting friends to our home. I met them at pubs or their houses, where I could relive the feeling of being at home I so missed, and relish the usual political discussions, not because, as some friends hinted, I was afraid she would be upset or angry, but because I loved her and believed in her right to choose her own friends and acquaintances and to have her own fun. We reached a reasonable agreement about my emotional attachment to Iraq and Iraqis and her disdain for them. We separated our married life and our professional concerns completely from my interest in politics. The most important thing was that we should accept each other for what we were. Until Suad saw the duck blackened by oil from the spill on British TV.

January 1991

There were lots of birds. One stood out with its long neck, heavy body, and two small wings. It looked like a duck, and they called it "Duck." Duck was covered in oil spill. She lifted her head up weakly, teetered, and struggled even to breathe, her neck twisting under the weight of the shining, thick oil spill clasping her feathers. She looked like a bronze creature rising out of savagely burning alluvial mud. She was unforgettable. Duck was everywhere, in the living room, on the TV screen, in news broadcasts, political debates, and environmental programs. Even the elderly zoologists were called out of their retirement at a moment's notice to talk about Duck's crisis. The UN representative spoke of Duck tearfully. An English traveler spoke regretfully of his past visits to the Ahwar Marshes in southern Iraq, saying, "Ducks were very happy there." Duck's picture appeared on the front page of every newspaper, serious or light, in the *Times*, *Independent*, *Guardian*, *Sun*, and *Daily Mirror*. War is clean. War is safe. The dead appear as moving targets on computer screens at first only to explode on TV screens later. War has no victims worthy of mention except for Duck, with her beautiful, twisted neck and her sad eyes.

Adnan and Suad

She sat glued to the TV after work. She did not move for hours. She watched every news program, on BBC1 at six, channel 4 at seven, BBC1 again at nine, ITV at ten, and BBC2 at ten-thirty. From a distance, Adnan, sitting on one of the huge armchairs, watched her long and hard.

Between the nine o'clock news and ten-thirty news, she turned, looked at him as if she was seeing him for the first time, and said, "What do you know about ducks?" He said, half in earnest and half in jest, "They fly, swim, and lay eggs. Their down covers a layer of fat that in turn protects them from fluctuating temperatures. Last but not least, according to our English friends, their meat tastes delicious if you know how to cook it. And, the best place for duck is a small restaurant in Chinatown."

She glared at him furiously and said a few nasty things as she usually did when she got angry. She turned her back on him and continued watching Duck's news. When he walked across the room in

to pick up the phone a few minutes later,
silently wiping tears away.

The room was charged with emotions. Hatred
hung heavily in the air. Who hated whom? Uncon-
sciously, he moved from the armchair to the couch,
then got up from the couch and walked back and
forth across the living room floor. She sat there, in
front of the TV, totally withdrawn. He wanted to talk
to her and to understand what really happened to her,
to him and between them. He wanted her to explain
her feelings, even if only her feelings toward Duck.
She kept silent, refusing to look up, and if she did, it
was only to throw reproachful looks his way. Why?

He picked up the phone violently and took it to
the bedroom. He closed the door behind him so as to
forget that she existed. He called his friend.

In a letter to his sister in Baghdad, even though
he knew very well he would not be able to send it—he
went on writing to her every day in the hopes that he
would be able to convince himself she was still alive
despite the relentless bombing—he wrote that night:
"The house is no longer big enough for the both of
us. We don't even look at each other anymore. She
has been sleeping in the guest room for weeks now. I
can't understand anything."

Ending 1

Like two tenants in a big English house, they avoid
meeting each other. If they should meet, God forbid,

they behave as if they were strangers. Good morning! Good morning! She does not look at him. He does not look at her. Goodbye! Goodbye! She is. He is. He comes. She goes. New meanings take shape. Nothing is meaningful.

One week later. The words they exchange are hateful. He chooses what he wants to hear. She chooses what she wants to hear. They choose words that make things worse, that scrape the scabs of their forgotten old wounds. She is talking to me scornfully, why? I can't stand his voice. Why don't I leave him? Cells of bitterness and anger multiply speedily. A swelling that keeps growing until it overwhelms every feeling. The heart practices aversion, silence, and growing apart.

Two months later. Duck flew. Quack! Quack! They cleaned her up from the oil spill. The bronze disappeared from her colors. Her neck straightened. She flew. Quack! Quack! A duck from a new battlefield replaced her on the TV screen and the front page of newspapers.

How do I calm the torment in my heart? I want to get close to her, to touch her, to ease the anger between us. I feel my skin tighten when I see him. I get tied up in knots inside. I can't breathe. Their meetings are painful moments. Every sentence they exchange, however short, turns into a fight. She rails at his emotional weakness. He rebukes her arrogance. He shouts, how many times do I have to tell you? She shouts back, how many times do I have to tell you?

The gulf between them grows wider after every fight. Do you even understand what you're saying, he yells. Why don't you face reality, she screams. Words, half uttered, explode between them like bombs, their shrapnel filling the air they take in and breathe out, charging around them like a wild bull. What did you say? The world has changed while you stood still. Your world is gone. You live in remote pasts, in the lands of once upon a time. He circles around her like a boxer blinded by punches. He wants to get out of the ring that has grown too small for them. She repeats in a loud voice: "Iraq is like you, living in the civilization of once upon a time." Silence.

One more month. Why don't we talk? Why don't we try to understand each other? Many people live in the same house without talking to each other. Silence. Why do I stay with him? I have my own work and friends. I live a different life. Why do I stay with him?

Round one thousand. Look at Japan. He does not hear her. How could you turn to the Americans to ask for aid for the people? In order to change them? She does not hear him. What democracy? What people are you talking about?

Another fight. You? He screams, as if spitting out an anger he has been repressing for years, you, do you know who the people are? Backward, how can I live with a backward man? You are backward. He steps toward her threateningly. How dare you talk to me like this? I am backward? Or is it the Shatt al-Wash-wash complex that is finally coming to the surface?

She looks at him in hate and disgust. He gets even angrier. She sees him barefoot, wearing a dirty *dishdasha*. She smells the stink of the creek. A fog of hate engulfs them from every direction. He comes near her. She pushes him away. She runs to the bathroom, horrified, to wash him off her body.

Ending 2

He feels her presence in the room. He looks up and sees her look at him in hate and disgust. His bitterness grows. She sees him barefoot, wearing a dirty *dishdasha*. She smells the stink of the creek. A fog of hate engulfs them from every direction. He comes near her and she pushes him away. In horror she runs to the bathroom to wash him off her body.

The reader may choose the ending she deems appropriate.

n.d.

5

Day

She spoke. I dreamt of an octagonal pool with mosaic edgings this morning. It is in the courtyard of our house in Baghdad. It is enveloped in strange plants with shiny foliage. I come near the pool. The water is clear. It is glittering. I see through the clear water a floor covered in arabesque. I think I see writing. I want to decipher it. I trace the lines, *La ilah . . . La ilah . . . illa Allah . . .* I squat near the edge. I put my face nearer the water. I squint, *La ilah . . . La ilah . . . illa Allah . . .* A little gold fish jumps out of the letters. More fish, of all colors and sizes, silver, red, black, and gold, big and small, leap out of the letters. They move fast. They turn, push and shove, and go around in circles. They fill the pool. I cannot see the bottom anymore. The pool is a mass of disjointed substance. I feel a hand on my shoulder. I turn around. I see my father, who passed away ten

From *Beyond Our Horizon* (1997), 93–95.

years ago. He is wearing his white *dishdasha* robe and smelling of rose water.

She thought, it must be Friday. Father perfumes himself with rose water before he heads out for the Friday prayer. He studies me as I watch the fish. We form an equilateral triangle, my father, the fish, and I. I want him to contemplate with me the moving mass, but he fixes his eyes on me, me alone, and looks ahead, far away from where I am. He frightens me. Like a child seeking attention, I turn and point to the pool. All the fish are now motionless, swollen, and floating on the surface of the green, putrid pool water. Tears fall down my face. I want to tell my father how cruel the whole thing is. I turn toward him. He is already on his way out.

He spoke. I dreamt of an octagonal pool with mosaic edgings this morning. It is in the middle of a place reminiscent of Tahrir Square in Baghdad. It is enclosed in ruins, crumbled buildings, abandoned shops, and restaurants and cafés empty of customers. The feel of a sandstorm hangs heavy in the air. The pool glitters like a gushing spring. It is lined with arabesque. A fish emerges from the letters, then another, and finally five. They move slowly. Their eyes stare at me. Out of nowhere a crowd of small children swarm me. Barefoot. Their faces are dirty, so are their *dishdasha* robes. They stretch out their hands toward the pool and try to catch the fish. They grab them by the tail and smack their head on the ground one after another. Blood splutters. I look at them. I see their faces and *dishdasha* robes covered in blood. The pool water is red. The sky is red.

I wake up. Breathless. I hear myself weep.

n.d.

6

Refuge

She stays put in her place all hours of the day, from eight in the morning till seven in the evening. Where can she go the rest of the twenty-four hours? She reaches her corner slowly, dragging her feet, suitcase, and bags, and lugging a heavy head screwed firmly to a neck above broad shoulders wrapped in a thick scarf. Thin hair, like white fuzz, barely covers her balding head.

She stops at every shop window on her daily journey. She sees her life pass before her eyes among the displayed cameras and lenses at Jessop Camera, or Starship Enterprise and the aliens on board at Forbidden Planet, or computers and laser printers at Computer World.

She makes a stop at every landmark on her way. The man behind the newspaper kiosk teases her. He asks her about her night. Was it red hot? She does not answer. She fixes her big green eyes on him for a

From *Beyond Our Horizon* (1997), 61–65.

few seconds. She shuffles on. Her swollen legs are like sponge cakes dipped in milk.

She makes it to her headquarters, every passer-by's sidewalk, where she deposits her bulky form and its paraphernalia: a suitcase and a large bag packed full with more bags. Leaning on the wall of a closed bank, she sits on the suitcase and watches the cash machine negotiate with the customers in writing before it dispenses cash to them.

Her perch is a meter away from the cash machine. With a shadow of a smile on her face, she keeps a vigil of the people and cars moving before her eyes, and of the different people who line up in front of the cash machine. Soot, dust, street pollution, and fumes coming out of car exhausts cloud the fair skin of her face. She puts her hand on the bag-lined-with-bags to make sure they are safely nearby.

She has a McDonald's breakfast every morning at ten thirty. A muffin sandwich of egg and bacon in a little white box from which an advertisement clown bursts out laughing when she opens the box. The McDonald's breakfast is served at every branch for only ninety-nine pence. She bites into it slowly and chews dutifully. She dips a scrap of bread into the soft egg yolk with her fingertips yellow with nicotine and black with dirt.

"Good morning!"

A tourist takes her photograph. She picks up a McDonald's paper cup from the ground with a mittened hand. She raises the cup in answer.

"To your health!"

Between slow sips her voice rings out sharp and thin. It penetrates the ears of the passers-by, enters their brains, and runs through their bodies. A loud voice, louder than the noises the passers-by and cars make, sings its own tune, letting slip only what is necessary.

"A penny for the needy!"

She repeats it every hour of the day.

"A penny you don't need."

She leans on the wall of the bank, her back to the passers-by; she turned her back on them a few years ago.

The shrill voice coming out of her back gives an unwelcome jolt to the passers-by. It has become an integral part of her body. The only sentence she whistles from the depth of her throat is the only sign of life coming out of her unmoving body. What surplus? Who has any extra money?

No one responds. The call is for everyone and for no one in particular. No one looks at her directly. They catch sight of her through the corner of their eye. They do not miss a beat.

She hugs the wall. A gray heap against a gray background shrouded in heaven's gray overcoat. The tattered suitcase is black, and the bag-lined-with-bags is gray. On the corner of Tottenham Court Road and Oxford Street, she holds herself up against the wall with her right hand and carries her suitcase with her left. The bag sits on the ground next to her. How old is she?

She pushes herself forward against the wall, as if she were looking out of a balcony only to find herself bumping into a protective iron wall. She sees before her eyes a magnificent scene. White buildings are shining in the sun. The smell of a sea nearby perfumes the air. She looks at the wall, her back to the passers-by. She narrows her eyes and looks intently as if she wants to see clearly through the wall.

"What does she want?"

The road ahead of her is a cement wall. She lifts her bloated hands with jutting veins and swollen joints carefully lest she disturb her own balance. She pulls at her scarf caught between her face and the wall and scraps of paint fall. Will life sprout from under the paint, from under the concrete skin? She is caught between two walls pressing against her distorted body mass. Her fingers scratch on the cement. She writes invisible words.

"Someone kissed her once."

Her body trembles. Her heart quakes. She drops her suitcase. She extends her hand. She rests on the wall. She disappears into the grains of its cement. She hides her eyes. She hides them from everybody. What she does not see, or what her eye cannot see, does not exist. What the passers-by avoid does not exist.

She moves her fingers slowly. Her eyes are closed. She sees what others do not see. She lives elsewhere.

She sculpts in the dark. The sky darkens in her hands. Darkness rolls into a ball at her fingertips. She feels the cold in the raindrops of darkness.

She wakes. She bends her back. She picks up the suitcase with one hand and with the other the bag-lined-with-bags. The same smile is on her face. She staggers under the weight of what she sees. She walks ahead, hiding behind her body.

n.d.

7

Turnstile

He looked at her with tears in his eyes and said: "This is the worst day of my life!"

She was on her way to work. As she began to walk down the steps of the West Hempstead Tube Station, she heard the train on her twenty-seventh step, the sound of distant vibrations and electrical flashes following on from steel wheels grinding against iron tracks. She came face to face with him as he descended the very same steps backward, with his back to the platform. She could still feel his face on hers.

Like a rag doll stuffed with sand and pebbles, he was holding onto the banister with all the might in his two hands, trying to use the upper half of his body to lift the bottom half then place it bit by bit on the next step.

"This is the worst day of my life!" he said in a trembling voice.

From *Beyond Our Horizon* (1997), 69–70.

She avoided him. She averted her eyes. She went past him quickly. Impatient bodies around her were hurling themselves down the steps. Time was ticking away one fast second following another. She curled up her body to squeeze through tight spaces. Her arm brushed against the sleeve of his coat when they passed each other. A shudder. Total disgust. She shrank further into herself, and in even more haste raced down the steps, tired and half asleep still, with the surging crowd. She fixed her eyes on the back of the crowd ahead of her and joined them on the platform just in time to see the train pull into the station.

n.d.

8

Cave

Village

He lived, until 1937, an ordinary life. He worked in his grandmother's shop for a few hours every day, from nine in the morning until one in the afternoon, then from four until seven in the evening, and spent the rest of his time enjoying the slow rhythm of living in the village. Everyone in the village followed the same routine. Unlike citizens of other villages though, they did not get up early in the morning, nor did they go to bed early at night.

Why did they call the place "the village"? He had no idea. Perhaps because they did not know how to define its identity and "the village" was the first thing that came to their mind when they watched it grow from five households to ten.

The village was in a remote corner far from the war. Four young villagers were conscripted into the army to defend the homeland. One of them was his

From *Beyond Our Horizon* (1997), 31–46.

father, who left him under his grandmother's care to join his unit faraway. It was a world war, and the fires of conflict raged around the globe. He was one year old. They did not hear of his father's death until months after the end of the war, when big trucks came through the village to pave its main road.

No one knew why this had to be done. They said it happened after long discussions and in anticipation of the breakout of another war. For twenty years, and amid neglect and lack of maintenance, herds of sheep and goats rambled on its asphalt surface alongside lorries carrying agricultural products and the lone postal van. Edges of the asphalt began to fall away, causing damage to the postal van, and the surface caved in everywhere, breaking the legs of unsuspecting sheep and goats.

A postman his father's age, if his father were still alive, arrived at the village in his postal van late morning every Monday, bringing all the goods his shop needed, from sugar, tea, sweets, and flour to candles, paraffin, combs, pots and pans, buttons, and thread spools. These in addition to the newspapers from the week before and, of course, letters.

The arrival of the postal van on Monday suited the villagers. They would have had plenty of time to anticipate what the post would bring, and would have talked about their hopes during the long hours of leisure over the two-day weekend at the café. They took pleasure in waiting and guessing but were always content with the regular mail they received in the end.

Letters, though rather few, were a richer source of news and discussion than the newspapers. Newspapers brought news of strange worlds with little relevance to anyone they knew. They would read the news and talk about it, then swiftly forget about it. But they paid close attention to the obituary page, taking great care to read the names of the dead and those of their relatives. They looked for anyone they knew dead or alive. Letters, especially the parts read aloud at the café, became the property of all. They poured over the lines written by familiar hands again and again, finding in them a cause for lengthy discussions. They carefully went over implications and ramifications as they formulated in their heads replies to the letters.

The postal van collected letters at the same time. It picked up many from the village shop, and more as it wound its way up and down the mountains. Those who lived too far from the main road, in places the postal van could not reach, would deposit their letters in small wood boxes hanging on tree branches bending over the main road.

They were still talking about his father at the café. They remembered him well nineteen years after his death. They did not remember his mother though. Perhaps it was not appropriate to talk about women in public places even after their death. He was different. He chose to speak about his mother, his beautiful and kind mother, who helped everyone around her, and about her lovely scent. Was there a link between human nature and her scent? He spoke about her with a love and longing that astonished his listeners, for he had never seen his mother. She died giving birth to him.

He had heard so much about her, from the stories his grandmother and the village women told, that he imagined he had seen her, tasted her milk, and slept in her arms. He would even correct his grandmother when she confused some details in the stories she told about her daughter.

He did not go to the café often. He preferred to spend his evenings with his grandmother. In her old age she could no longer move as before, and her body had become so frail it easily sustained breaks and injuries. He wanted to protect her from harm, as she did when he was a child, following him everywhere he went.

When he strolled through the door connecting the shop and the house in the afternoon and evening he would find her sitting in a corner knitting for him a pullover, a pair of socks, a hat, or whatever struck her fancy. He would prepare a meal for the both of them, sit with her, exchange stories with her, or read to her. He reread to her every news item in the old newspapers she had kept, and every line in the ten-volume *History of the World* his father left behind. Even though these had lost their luster through constant repetition, he continued to be attentive to them, as he would his grandmother's stories.

On the occasions he went to the café, he listened to the radio equally attentively, to the dull reports on the weather, harvest, migrants, young people's desire to leave the village, and even matchmaking.

A tourist who lost his way wandered into the café once. He announced he was a traveler, for he disliked being called a tourist. He told them about the world, and they told him about their days. They drank to the health of the traveler sweet wine distilled from white grapes and perfumed with wild anise. He discussed politics and history with them and was astounded by how much they knew about the world. Respecting their wish to stay far from the others, he apologized for his early impressions and bid them a grateful farewell.

The population of the village was about fifty. They lived in twenty houses built without prior planning or permission on the two sides of the main road, a farm, a shop, and a café, which was really an odd extension of one of the houses. It was made up of mainly the old, the middle-aged, and children. Young men were missing from the village age groups. They could not stay still and preferred to go where there was action and variation, to the cities.

Mountain

He was twenty-four. He chose to stay, to be near his grandmother, her shop, and the mountains surrounding his village. The tallest of them was more

than 1,100 meters above sea level. This was the mag-
net that pulled him, more than anyone else, toward
rocks and away from people. Or perhaps it drew him
even closer to them, to their stable nature and tranquil life.

He would spend hours climbing the mountain
and sitting on a rock high up there to contemplate
and dream. He turned to his inner self fully awake,
retreating into her, and into the wild grass, saplings,
and trees to which she belonged. He would stand
up tall, lifting his face to the falling snowflakes in
the winter. In the spring, he would lie on the grass,
stretch out his body and look at the clouds drifting
across the heaven, chameleons in a world secure in
its constancy.

To be at one with nature is to accept her as she
is, to be alive among her elements, to partake in the
varying chapters of her life, awake or in slumber,
sunny or stormy, cold or warm, rain or snow, harvest
or drought, and to be so in love with her you become
her twin and change the tones of your skin according
to the colors of her seasons: dark, shadowy, light.

There were four boxes of watercolors on a shelf
in the right corner of his shop. They had remained
there untouched for years. It never occurred to anyone to ask for watercolors. The children, all nine of
them, who walked for miles to class in the neighboring village, got their supplies of notebooks, pencils
and pens, and uniforms from their school. They wore

their uniforms with enthusiasm at the beginning of the school year, but they would soon enough hide them and claim to have lost them.

The four boxes of watercolors were forgotten in their corner on the shelf until one frigid winter evening he decided to bring one down and take it to the living room. He drew colorful lines on white paper and on pages whose colors had gone off, and spilled paint over their edges. A few days later, he learned to control his force and lighten his touch. He put the box of watercolors and papers in a cloth bag he carried with him regularly on his walks. He did not know how to draw shapes very well, but his knowledge of nature helped him to understand colors. He wanted to transfer the colors of the mountains to paper, to capture them, to hold them captive, and take them to his living room and show them to his grandmother so as to brighten her long evening hours.

The mountains bordering the village were rich with perfumed vegetation, from groves of thyme, oregano, and rosemary to thickets of sumac, fig, and olive. The oldest olive tree in these mountains was nature's gift to humanity. It had enormous roots and a hollowed trunk the size of a room big enough for four people to stand in. It was without a roof or a ceiling. Only ants and worms lived in it. Branches green with leaves and heavy with fruits grew out of its wrinkled, thick elephant skin artlessly, like a sermon delivered impulsively.

It drizzled. It poured. The earth sipped, gulped, and swallowed instantly. It kept its rain harvest out of sight and safe in the deep recesses of her innermost core. Her surface was fertile with lemon, orange, almond, and carob trees. A chorus of sounds coming from the trees, animals, birds, and his solitary presence filled the mountain air. It was singing the sound of silence.

He learned to listen, to listen to the sound of silence in the mountains, to the sound of nature, to the insects buzzing about, the bird wings bustling above, and the tree leaves rustling all around. With the breeze on his face, he lay still, listening to life rising up slowly from the gut of the tree, to form another layer in her timber, and add one more year to her age.

Her silent tunes changed with her colors, all in step with the budding of flowers following the withering of trees and the stirrings of spring in the wake of winter slumber. Colors were born in the big thaw. As snow turned into streams and seeped deep into the earth, life rose up from her heart and blossomed on her face. She was reborn amid budding flowers and breeding animals.

His daily wanderings, accompanied by tunes filling his ears and colors dazzling his eyes, brought him close to his mountain. He wanted more from her, as he drew, to get even closer, to know her intimately, to touch her soul, and to understand the meaning of their existence together, of his life.

Cave

He reached the summit one day. A blue rock caught his eye. Its magnificence astounded him. He drew near and saw a mass of blue flowers covering its entire surface. He touched them. He breathed in their fragrance. A sudden feeling that they were hiding something behind them took hold of him. He tried to push at them, and after some effort he moved them sideways. An opening through which he could crawl inside revealed itself to him. He was possessed by the sense of awe usually felt by someone on the edge of an abyss about to fall into an unfathomable void. He moved the rock back to its place. It was time for him to go home.

He entered the cave the day after. His body trembled from the silence of his anticipation. The lamp in his hand lit up the belly of nature. The granules of air hung on invisible threads. He groped along the passage narrowing here and widening there. The walls were so soft to his touch he could even feel himself melt inside. He lifted the lamp and saw marble all around him. It was decorated by overlapping forms so alive they were almost moving.

Deep inside the cave water was dripping gently, one slow drop after another, in corridors of varying sizes that did not seem to be a part of the mountain. Stalagmite formations, like sand dunes, rose up from the center of the earth in curves and waves, and stalactite formations, also like sand dunes, hung down from the ceiling, also in curves and waves. They rarely met midair. The ceiling and floor were smooth surfaces, and the walls sprouted formations that competed with those rising up from the floor or hanging down from the ceiling. Colors differed from one corridor to another because of the different ingredients that went into their making. It was red here because marble mixed with iron, green there because it mixed with calcite, and black because it mixed with moss. No two formations looked alike. Every square centimeter of the rock formations, deposits of minerals accumulated with every drop of water, needed one hundred years of still air and fixed temperature. There was no room for any man to add his signature to the cave.

He discovered something new every time he visited. His eyes became accustomed to darkness. There was light in the dark, and his eyes got used to the cave and no longer needed the lamp to see. The pupils in the wide opened eyes turned into the colors of the rock formations. They transformed the forms into knowledge that opened secret doors to the mystery he was witnessing. A total existence he had been longing to experience since he did-not-know-when. His vision had been limited by what the eye could see before he discovered the cave. The formations he saw before were sublime in their own ways: people standing up, sitting down, lying back, raising their hands in prayer, "*Allahu akbar*!," prostrating in supplication, pleading for mercy and forgiveness. The shape of a woman stood at the center of a quiet place in the cave. A transparent veil covering her from hair down revealed the fine features of her face. She was looking down with love at the shape of a child she was holding to her breast. The very serenity of mother and child was threatened by stalactite formations above her head: needles of uneven length, each the size of an obelisk, were pointing at them.

The cave removed the barrier between the eye and what it saw. He became one with nature. He now saw clearly that his translucent inner world illuminated the world outside. The cave became his inner world two years after his daily visits. Conversing with the cave in a common language only they knew, he reached a point when he saw and heard everything, not just what his eye and ear chose for him.

In the days and months he made his daily journey to the cave, he wandered around the passages and gave the rock formations names he thought suited them. This was the "Romantic Mansion," that was the "Gateway to Hell," "Paradise," the "Enchanted City," and "Elephant." "Elephant" was a gigantic animal formation he leaned on to avoid falling when he was navigating the slippery ground awash with marble waves. He saw through his senses. He saw the dripping water and what it created. He saw air. He saw labyrinths in the shape of domes, alleys, canals, and hallways. He saw life as he had never seen before. He felt life as he had never felt before. The rock formations animated life for him and he held on to it, translating the lines of dripping water and the colors of rock formations into his own watercolors.

Grandmother

His retreat did not last very long. He had to return to his grandmother. She lasted a year on her deathbed. He watched her take her leave unhurriedly, retreating into her diminishing body first, then drifting out of her mind. As she slipped into a fathomless darkness, she recited religious hymns in delirium and called out to her mother like a frightened child. Did wisdom grow against the grain of the dwindling body, as it moved less, felt less, and savored less with the steady onslaught of illness? What of thought and memory? Could we learn to be wiser without our memory, the roadmap left for us by our past?

His grandmother's skin grew increasingly translucent with the passage of time, and her kind face became a mass of unpredictable lines. With the breakdown of the vehicle of her soul, she lost her knowledge of everything else. She stopped talking to him, complaining about her solitary existence or calling him to help her. She lived in another world. Did she also find her cave?

He abandoned his cave for her sake. He stopped painting. He opened the shop no more than two hours per day. The presence of death in his living room painfully awakened in him senses he felt he had to ruminate on for a long time before he could untangle their jumbled threads as he would the yarn in his grandmother's basket. Without winding each around a spool according to its color, he would not be able to grasp the meaning of death or accept it.

He spent his days awaiting his grandmother's death. He woke up in the morning expecting her to have left her tired, disintegrating body. The gift of life was an unfair deal, he felt, for from its very first moment it was conditioned by death. Man worked, went to war, traveled, loved, procreated, thought, wept, felt joy, and built, all the while holding on to death's hand, day and night, not knowing when it would pull him toward it.

Courageous, man was, and naive!

War

The day he and three others received their conscription letters calling them to the battlefront to defend their homeland in a world war, he smiled. They made the decision he had been hesitating to make. With tears of joy in his eyes, he packed his belongings, handed his house and store keys to his neighbor, bid farewell to his fellow villagers, and left ecstatically for his cave.

He gave in to her call and went inside. He heard his heart beat with every drop of the water dripping down from the ceiling and along the surface of the rock formations. He could at times hear the beating in the marble veins as if it were the music of a soundless string ensemble. His ability to see, hear, and feel grew with the time he spent in the cave.

He moved from one place to another every day, changing the angle of his view and hearing. The inside of the cave was different from its outside. The light of life emitted from the unmoving rock formations, brightening up the imagination and expanding her world beyond the walls of the cave. She picked up the colors of the universe, colors the eye could not tally, colors that sparkled, shimmered, and dazzled, colors that united life with death.

One drop following another, he looked, he saw, he received, he recorded, he perceived, he realized. Joy filled him. Light suffused him. He rose above and beyond place. One drop of water following another fell on him. He turned into a glittering diamond, a splendid body of light whose sparkles graced all the inhabitants of the cave.

n.d.

From *There Is Such Other* (1999)

9

Pilgrimage

The House

Sheila stood at the gate of the small house that looked like a hut built in the wrong place. Five tourists disembarked from the bus right behind her: a Swiss man, a French man, a Dutch man, and an English man and his wife. Sheila, our guide from the Swansea Literary Tours, pointed to the blue round plaque fitted on the front wall of the house, between two windows on the first floor, and said: "This is his house." She touched the front door painted in white and said, "He looked out to the sea from here, and contemplated the ebbs and flows." One asked, "What is the house number?" "Five." "What is the name of the street?" "Cwmdonkin Drive." "Pardon?" "C. w. m. d. o. n. k. i. n." Like a fatigued employee, Sheila spelled out the name of the street mechanically.

They stood quietly for a few minutes in front of the door. They turned their backs to it and looked

From *There Is Such Other* (1999), 9–18.

ahead, trying to imitate what the poet used to do, so as to see the sea and its ebbs and flows. They saw nothing. The newly erected houses on both sides of the street blocked their view. They felt a momentary sadness. They were deprived of a means of getting close to the poet. One of the rituals of their pilgrimage to him was sabotaged. To compensate for their loss, they turned around to contemplate the little house one more time. The Frenchman commented: "Baudelaire said something about the amazing effect of looking at something at length. Whatever we spend time contemplating for a long time always becomes interesting." Everybody laughed except for him. He looked rather sad.

They walked toward the bus. Ghada said: "This neighborhood reminds me of High Gate in London." The German asked her with great concern: "Are you homesick?" "No, not at all! It's my way of getting to know a new place. If I compare it with places I know well I won't forget it." "You'll miss something important if you do this," the German responded, "You won't feel the excitement of discovery because you'll be transforming new places into familiar ones. If you do this you won't feel the need to discover the new place." Taken aback, Ghada looked at him quizzically. "All I said was that this place reminded me of a neighborhood I know." He continued, heedless of her protest, "All places, for you, regardless of where you go, become one and the same." She muttered in her English husband's ear, cursing him for making her accompany him on this literary journey.

They returned to their seats and the bus set off. After a long silence, heavy like air saturated with humidity, Ghada began to speak. She would have to initiate a conversation, she thought, if she wanted to make the four coming days with these visitors to the poet's city bearable. "Did I tell you about my dream last night?" She went on, not waiting for anyone to respond. "It was a strange dream. I felt an invisible force drawing me toward it. I was hanging on to everything I could find around me to fight off this terrific magnetic force. I was screaming at the top of my lungs, refusing to go, no, no, I don't want to go with you. What I got back was an even more powerful pull, and a mysterious voice, more like echoes than anything else. I was hearing this voice intertwined with the force as rising and falling waves."

Ghada went silent. She was looking away into the distance as if she were trying to keep that mysterious power to herself. She realized suddenly that all eyes were on her and quickly brushed the memory away. "It was a terrifying dream." "Was it a dream or a nightmare?" "I don't know. How could I have known? I was very afraid." Another asked, "Was it a ghost?" "Do you believe in ghosts?" "No, of course not," he laughed out loud, "I believe in hidden forces, unknown forces created by gravity and energy that find their way to those inexplicable extraordinary phenomena. But ghosts," he laughed out loud, "these are creatures of a befuddled mind. They talked a lot about ghosts haunting the castles and abandoned mansions we visited but believe you me none materialized in all the nights I stayed up waiting to catch a glimpse of them." The Frenchman said, "Ghosts do not appear in solid forms. You feel them in the vibrations of the surroundings." "It is then the state of the mind created by the expectation for something specific." Ghada intervened to recover her role. "I don't think so. I felt the presence of a ghost in the Scottish castle we visited last year. I heard music. It was the ghost of a musician who lived in the castle. He was forced out of the castle and died in sorrow then returned to settle there."

Sheila waited patiently for them to finish their chitchat about ghosts. She politely brought their attention back to Dylan Thomas. "I know very well that the time is short. We won't have time to see all the places the poet lived in or wandered about, but I think it is very important for you to see the place he mentioned in that famous poem, 'The Hunchback in the Park.'" Sheila left the bus. The tourists followed. She led them to a beautiful park that looked like a palm spread across the breast of a woman. Neatly trimmed. A fountain stood in the middle. Leaves looking like flowers floated on its water. A small brook ran nearby. Sheila said to those standing around her, "He used to sit here," pointing to a place,

"This was his favorite place." The group drew near a drinking fountain, a very ordinary fountain like any other they had seen in other parks, neglected, rusty, and dry. They looked at it in veneration. "It needs refurbishing," Ghada whispered. "Yes," Sheila replied, "the faucet and basin will be restored after this year's celebration of Dylan Thomas's birth." They stood around the fountain. They contemplated it at length. Lingering in the places the poet loved and wrote about meant they had some of what their poet had, which would eventually allow them to possess the poet. The German, his hand reaching out to the fountain and his fingertips caressing the mouth, whispered in a dreamy voice, "Drinking from a cup chained to the fountain." "He stole the cup," Sheila said, "and the metal chain that locked the cup to the fountain too."

A man passed by on a motorcycle. They turned their heads in his direction. He looked at them absent-mindedly. Ghada put her hand on her heart and drew a deep breath. "Did you see what I saw," she said, "doesn't he look just like Dylan Thomas?" Sheila interrupted, trying to finish what she had started. "He spent hours and hours in the park, alone, reading, writing, walking, and of course drinking." Ghada said to Michael as they made their way toward the bus, "These houses are beautiful." "Yes, because they look over the park." "They remind me of houses overlooking the Cornwall coast."

The Pub

They sat to drink beer in a well-lit corner of the pub while their lunch was being prepared. Pictures of Dylan Thomas in different stages of his life hung on the walls. They looked around silently. "Is this his favorite pub?" Ghada asked. "No," Sheila replied, "one of his favorite pubs. Whichever pub served him alcohol was his favorite. He chased after his drink wherever he went." "How did he make a living?" "Dylan Thomas was a professional beggar. He took from people whatever he could get out of them. His family went through very difficult times because of him. But he always succeeded in getting what he wanted, using his name and his status as poet."

A trembling, breathless voice rose from somewhere near the bar, a bit of a distance from them, a voice of a drunk that broke Ghada's heart:

> The hunchback in the park
> A solitary mister
> Propped between trees and water
>
> Slept at night in a dog kennel
> But nobody chained him up.

Ghada looked around her. Her heartbeat quickened. She was looking for a face that matched the voice she knew so well from the recordings she had listened to time and again. She saw a man, standing, in a dark corner, swaying, waving his arms, and bowing to the applause of a phantom audience. He did not finish the poem.

"How did he die?" the Dutchman inquired. "He died in New York after downing eighteen glasses of whiskey. 'Massive abuse of the body' is stated as the cause of death in his autopsy report." "Was the glass full," Ghada asked, "or did he drink eighteen units of whiskey?" "I don't exactly know." "What is the size of one unit of whiskey?" Ghada turned to her husband. "I don't know. I know it by sight not measurement." "Do you think it is 5 cc?" "Maybe." Sheila interrupted once again. "I think the best way is to measure by the standard whiskey glasses." Insistently, Ghada went on talking about the very same issue, as if knowing the exact measurement would help her solve an enigmatic, difficult problem. "Let's say that the double of each unit is 50. Multiply that by 18 and you get 900. It is less than a liter. I don't think it is a lethal dose, especially if we surmise that he drank it over a period of a few hours." Michael made a decisive intervention at this very moment in what he thought of as disturbance to others. "It is lethal if it was the dose he had been abusing his body with every night."

The Museum

A hall dedicated to the commemoration of the poet. His pictures. His notebooks. His things. Stage designs.

His books. His voice, inebriated, overwhelmed the place, scattering a poem, one line after another, on the visitors, completing a poem whose beginning they heard in another place, as if he were reminding them that he would be with them wherever they went.

A middle-aged woman entered the hall. Petite, pale, her hair blond streaked with silver. Quietly, she sat behind a table and waited for the visitors to gather around her. On the wall behind her the pictures of her father and mother hung, as well as her childhood pictures with her brothers. Someone turned off the recording. The sudden jarring silence reminded them of the absence of that special familiar someone. Everybody looked around them, remembering that they were in a public place. They were not, as they had thought, alone with the voice of the poet.

The daughter of the poet swept through the visitors with exhausted eyes that had given in to the burden placed on her. A carnival of many nationalities brought together here by her iconic father, his poetry, his abuse of alcohol, his self-destructive streak, and his premature death. Because she was his daughter, they shrouded her in holiness with a translucent veil. They sat before her, peering, looking in her face for the features of their idol. She sat there quietly, waiting for questions. She toyed with the papers in front of her, like a child, with her father's poems. She raised her head. She picked a face in the front row to fix her eyes on and start the conversation, the face of a woman, an Oriental woman, which reminded her of her recent visit to Istanbul University, where she read some of her poems translated into Turkish. "Does anyone want to ask me about anything specific?"

Silence.

Dylan Thomas was everywhere in the hall, in the person of his daughter, in his pictures, and his things scattered around the hall in a very organized fashion. The echoes of his voice were in their heads, growing even louder through his daughter's voice.

"It's not easy being Dylan Thomas's daughter. It is a burden I finally gave in too after much resistance. It took a very long time for me to accept it. I didn't choose to represent my father. I was pushed into it. The insistence of people pushed me into it, and my two brothers' refusal to attend events having anything to do with him, even when they erected his statue to honor him in Wales. My brothers refused to go and I had to go on my own. They hate being known as his sons."

"Shall I tell you about his poetry? His poetry is lyrical. His voice was lyrical. He created a new poetic language. Philip Larkin and Ted Hughes followed in his footsteps. He talked magically about ordinary subjects in his poems and plays: life, death, and nature. He is described as a Welsh poet but in truth he didn't know the Welsh language at all. His mother tongue was English. His father forbade him from speaking Welsh since he was a child because he, i.e. the father, admired the English language and thought it would be the language of the future. This was how he became the most important Welsh poet, a stranger to his own language and an innovator in the language of strangers."

"What about my mother?"

Her voice quivered when she talked about her mother.

"My mother was very attractive. She thought he was a genius. But she didn't like to listen to what he wrote, particularly because he wanted to monopolize her attention. He loved to read his poems aloud and would repeat the line he liked tens of times. He liked how they echoed in the kitchen and in the bathroom. She would kick him out and send him to the garden."

She then lowered her voice and sweetly said, as if confessing a secret to the eyes gazing at her in admiration, Ghada's eyes, "Every time I talked about him I saw him with fresh eyes and his picture would change." Her seductive eyes in a dream, she revealed something even more profound, "I began to feel attracted to my father. I felt I was getting closer to him. I understood him when I read his poems aloud to an audience, because I was reading what I knew, what I lived as a child, in his shadow. Slowly but steadily I recovered his voice, intoxicated, sad, glittering in happiness, drowning in isolation, high on admiration of others' voices. I recovered my father." Her voice rose and fell, giddy with happiness, drunk, mournful, and high, as she spoke the last words.

Ghada's eyes filled with tears. She felt, like in her dream, a force pulling her toward something accompanied by a voice that gave her body goose bumps. She could no longer resist. She gave in to the eyes that could see through her, to that moment of private confession, to the words, to the voice of the commanding poem resurrected from a fragile body.

All night in the unmade park
After the railings and shrubberies
The birds the grass the trees the lake
And the wild boys innocent as strawberries
Had followed the hunchback
To his kennel in the dark.

n.d.

10

Painting

The exhibition would go on for a month, the organizer told her. She said to her son that a month was not a long time, I'll keep watch in the morning and you'll come in the afternoon. He burst out in sudden anger, waving his right hand violently, as if he wanted to push his father away, far away from him. "What about him? Why doesn't he come himself? The paintings are his, aren't they?"

She felt tired. A sudden fatigue, like her son's anger. Nervous exhaustion from unending repetition. From years of being stranded between two charging bulls, the son and the father. Both accused her of weakness, of being obliging to the other. She sensed the coming on of another battle in which she would be the sure loser. She was stuck between two people who refused to move even a tiny inch from their position. She could tell from her son's convulsive words, from his addressing his father in the third

From *There Is Such Other* (1999), 41–46.

person. She could feel the rising heat of his stubborn rejection.

She gazed at his face placidly, holding down her temper, and said, quietly repeating what she had been saying to him hundreds of times for so many years, as if she were saying the words for the first time: "Your father doesn't like to mix with people but I do. This is not complicated at all. Why do you complicate things? I also enjoy having you with me." She added, pleading, "At least do it for my sake." "One day you will beg people to come and see his paintings as well," he whispered, looking at her lovingly, "and I'm sure they will come, for your sake."

A feeling of warmth enveloped her. His simple words wiped away her fatigue. He was still able to express his love for her with a childlike innocence even though he, in his twenties, had long left his childhood behind. Hanging paintings on temporary walls was not really a difficult task, but she wanted him with her because she really enjoyed his company. It was her way of getting him to spend time with her, even if only for a few minutes.

The preparations were complete. Two sets of temporary wood walls in gray paint, one erected along the church wall and the other along the colossal southern columns of Covent Garden, marked out the exhibition space. The participating artists hung their paintings on these walls every morning and took them down every evening for storage in the church overnight. Five refugee artists from different countries took part in the London event. The exhibition, called *Bend*, was a collated European-wide effort in which parallel events took place at the same time in other cities. The artists, all five of them, sat on folding chairs with their backs to their paintings and their faces to Covent Garden's courtyard.

Here, in London's center for tourism, clowns were trying to make the tourists laugh. Masses of colorful clothes, skins, and features. Comedians performed silent sketches for a silent audience. Commotions of people coming and going, milling about, and drinking, eating, and chatting in cafés and restaurants generously fill the space. Who was watching whom? Three women mimes stood in the middle of the square. One moved. The onlookers screamed in admiration and amazement. Cameras clicked in nonstop succession as they tried to capture the fleeting moments of wonder before they disappeared even from memory. An African musical troupe played a rhythmic tune, and those standing around swayed with its beats. The church and the exhibition were the tranquil background against which the clamor of people enjoying life unfolded.

Another kind of life was churning in the day-care center at the far end of the church. Fathers brought half-asleep children in the morning, and mothers picked them up fully awake and frenziedly active in the afternoon. "If we were living in normal circumstances," she whispered to her heart, "I would have had six children." She sighed, full of regret, her eyes tearing, how she loved children, she thought to herself. She used to hold her only son in her arms during the days he would allow it and say, "You are my six children." His will to fly away from her grew in proportion to her attachment to him.

"Arrange the paintings according to what you think best. I trust your taste," her husband said so as to sever his ties with the paintings and to be rid of the burden of her anxiety. He would begin to pursue another interest that would in the end give him a new painting. Nothing in his paintings attracted attention. Ten paintings in only two colors: white and black. A serene statement about an incomprehensible situation. The viewers must study them, with the same tranquility, and patiently work out their signs and symbols. These were his most recent works. He painted them in the aftermath of the US bombings of Iraq, when he was possessed by anger and impotence, so he painted his anger, impotence, love, grief, and fear. He painted his feelings. He saw with his mind's eye scenes, in white and black, of collapsed buildings, lands stripped bare, bombing targets, ruins, and falling bridges.

The only variable in the paintings is the shades. They are thick and in darker hues than the shapes he drew tentatively at the beginning when he thought he could see them but which he later abandoned, leaving them, like him, impotent. The background was gray. Holes. Openings. Severed lines. The city was a vast arena of ruins, inhabited by citizens carrying her ruins in their bodies. No indications of time or place. Familiar signs of inhabited cities were absent. Ruins, nothing but ruins, of the soul, of the city. Was it true that ruins begat ruins? The night was dark and the depressed prolonged its hours. He could not bear leaving the place of his pain, not even for brief moments, and sank into one abyss after another. His purpose was to reach the ultimate darkness so that he could rest forever.

She did not look at the paintings because she lived every moment of their making. She would occasionally lift her head from the book or newspaper she was reading and watch the viewers. She wanted to know their reactions. Did they see what she saw? How much of her husband's message did they get? Some took a quick glance and walked away. Perhaps the pain coming out of the paintings was too distressing for the happy man? Others turned their faces away from them. Only a few stood before them and contemplated, quietly, before they moved away in slow steps. Were they avoiding awakening a city in ruins?

In the first, second, and third weeks, they spoke to her. They asked her questions. They wanted to know about the artist and his city. She told them, in great excitement, about the paintings, and the rubbles of the city, for she felt she belonged to both. These were her paintings as much as they were his. She lived them. She inhaled the stinging smell of paints and witnessed his withdrawal from the world as he painted them. Sitting among his works, she turned into another white and black painting. Her complexion was pale white. Her long jet-black hair covered her shoulders. And the layers of black she wrapped around her thin body gave her a sizable presence.

A woman in her fifties stood long before the paintings in the second week. Bringing her face very close to the small painting carrying the number 4, she peered at it for quite a while. She then turned to her, congratulated her, "wonderful miniatures," and left. She was intrigued, put down the newspaper she was pretending to read, and walked up to the painting. She wanted to know what made the woman examine it with such concentration. She saw something new, two shapes that were not there before, a man and woman sheltering each other, holding each other close with what seemed like tens of arms. Their features were far from clear, but the heat being emitted from their bodies was enough to illuminate what was around them.

She told her husband that night about the stranger's admiration for the shapes of the man and woman he drew. He said nonchalantly that he did not draw the two shapes but if the woman saw these two shapes then it was her right to see what she wanted to see and therefore they must be there.

In the days that followed, the painting grew, gradually but steadily, and picked up more shades. It changed. It acquired a coarse surface with the feel of colors mixed with earth and half-melted rubber that gave it a new solidity and density and at the same time redistributed its shades. The two colors, white and black, multiplied into myriad shades of gray, silver, and milk. Its hues became eye-catchingly distinct. The polite quiet statement disappeared. A sigh, almost a scream, shot out of the grays, an open mouth the size of pain. The colors of rubber were now celestial movements taking place at the far end of the horizon. Moving clouds touched still clouds above mountain peaks under the heaven. The painting came breathtakingly alive, brushing off the layers of dust accumulated on its body and the city. Varying formations began to appear in the painting every day. She breathed in, through it, the air of the city ruins, and became one with the people living there, its rubble and remains. She felt the rock sitting heavily on her chest begin to crumble. She could breathe again.

Her son never came the entire month. She sat alone in the square crowded with thousands of people every day, in solitary confinement with the paintings. She no longer heard or saw what was happening around her. She spent her days cut off from the outside world. Her son finally came, on the last day of the exhibition, to help her pack the paintings. He arrived late and saw her standing there, on her own, before a huge mural he thought he had seen before. With eyes filled with tears, she explained to him what she saw: picking up from a conversation interrupted for a brief moment due to unforeseeable circumstances, and with a voice trembling with excitement and happiness, she deciphered for him the hieroglyphic symbols of the obelisk. Was this his mother, the woman who could not take any decisive sides between him and his father?

Like a priestess confident of what she knew, of what she saw, she pointed at the shapes floating above the ruins of the city pervading his father's paintings, which did not disappear but had acquired distinct features. People are the essence of the painting, his mother said. Places change. They may get better or worse. Places are the product of imagination, the priestess added, pointing to the light colors in the painting. Afire with passion, his mother had disappeared into an intoxicated trance and he was drawn into it very quickly, and into the painting following her unusually warm voice. The passion spread from his mother to the painting and from the painting to him. A strange force moved around the triangle from his mother to the painting then him. He had never felt so close to his mother before.

With her he owned the past, from the cradle to adulthood—a sperm in the womb, unsteady steps, first words, early tentative written letters, trips to places with his hand firmly held in hers. On the open ground of the wide square sitting in the heart of a city noisy with life, they stood alone, so close together their shoulders were touching, lost to the world, haloed by the heat of their passion.

n.d.

Packaged Life (2007)

11

Packaged Life

Episode One

Lanzarote, Canary Islands, October 1998

Act One

He was the first in line. He arrived at the airport three hours before the scheduled departure time. He stood in front of the empty check-in counters for an entire hour before the clerk began checking tickets and passports and weighing luggage. He asked her to put him in a window seat and in the area dedicated to nonsmokers. The clerk smiled and explained gently, "Smoking is prohibited on all our flights." He remembered an announcement to this effect. She handed his ticket and passport back to him. "Go to the waiting area. We will announce the departure gate half an hour before takeoff. It will appear on the monitors there."

Two hours of waiting. He had to kill time. He had to keep himself busy. He ate a tuna mayonnaise sandwich his parents prepared for him in the morning.

He drank an orange juice and threw the bottle in the rubbish bin. He went to the toilet. He washed his hands several times to get rid of the smell of tuna. He sat in a corner, away from the other passengers, watching planes take off and land behind an airport window. He pulled out the book she recommended to him from his hand luggage. He looked at it despondently then returned it to its place. He walked around in shops and cafés. He wanted to buy a bottle of perfume for her from the duty-free shop but remembered her warning and left the shop empty handed. He went to the toilet again. The smell of tuna seemed to have stuck to his hands. He sat in front of a monitor, staring, and waited for the announcement of the departure gate. The gate was finally open.

As soon as he settled into seat 6A next to the window he followed all the instructions lit above his seat. He adjusted the back of his seat, fastened his seatbelt, put his book in the seat pocket in front of him, and looked expectantly at the small screen installed on the ceiling, which everyone could comfortably see. When would the broadcast begin? The screen was dim, waiting for the plane to take off and reach a certain altitude. The man sitting next to him in 6B asked him, "Is this your first visit to Lanzarote?" He replied quickly, "No, no, it's my second." "Why? I mean why are you going back?"

They were interrupted by the voice of the flight attendant asking them to watch her while she demonstrated safety procedures. He must pay attention.

Her movements were mechanical. Her smile revealed her teeth and a bit of her gums. Her voice was clear. She repeated her instructions in easily understood language. She was like his teacher.

He replied distractedly, his eyes full of the flight attendant, "Birds." The friendly passenger next to him laughed out aloud, his laughter insinuating a manly solidarity. "You mean women, don't you? I do return to some of the places I have visited in spite of myself," he said, nudging him, "for the sake of birds, I mean women, the most beautiful women are birds, don't you think?"

The flight attendant put the oxygen mask on her mouth, pretending to breathe, and her teeth and gums disappeared. He felt the nudge and hastened with his answer. "No, not at all, I really meant birds, seagulls, white birds, they are lonely."

The flight attendant completed her demonstration, and he heard his neighbor mutter. Did he make him angry? Maybe he did. He felt sad. He wanted to make amends. He asked him in a friendly tone, "Do you want to hear about my dream?"

He waited.

He wanted to tell his neighbor about his dream, his recurring dream. The other shook his head no. Very politely the man buried his friendly initiative alive. He pulled out the airline magazine from the seat pocket in front of him. *Universe Packaged Tours Magazine.* "Maybe later," the stranger said as he turned the pages of the magazine.

When would the broadcast begin? The small screen was still dark, like a sky without stars. To keep himself occupied, he pulled out for the second, or was it the third time, he could not remember, *The Tales of the Prophets*, and opened it to the page he had marked by folding its edge, page 11, and looked at the words. No use. He looked up again at the screen. He saw reflections of distant lights flickering on it. He was completely absorbed until the voice of the flight attendant interrupted him again, "Would you like a set of ear phones? It's two pounds and a half and you can use it on all future Universe Airline flights." "No, thank you." The neighbor asked the flight attendant, as he handed over the cash, "What is today's film?" "*Chicken Run*. It is an animation film with Mel Gibson as the lead male voice." He guffawed teasingly, "Chicken Mel Gibson, what a wonderful title!" He shared in their laugh. The broadcast would begin soon then.

In Lanzarote, he was the first to exit the airport and the first to stand in line next to the bus. Bus no. 3 parked on tarmac no. 7 would deliver them to their hotels and apartments. He had no heavy luggage. His bag did not even weigh five kilos, and they let him take it with him on board the plane. He waited alone with the driver for forty-five minutes. When would the rest of the passengers arrive? The driver did not stop smoking. A cloud of smoke covered his face. He did not stop looking at his watch either. Were the arms moving?

Minute 48

He stood outside the bus. He watched the passengers drag their heavy suitcases toward the bus in front of him. He counted five, seven, ten . . .

Minute 60

The passengers arrived slowly. They occupied their seats on the bus. The representative of the company introduced himself to the tourists. "My name is David," he said, and counted the passengers on the bus, calling out their names. He laughed out loud all of a sudden. Everyone looked at him inquiringly. He lowered his head in embarrassment. He had silently counted the passengers with David, imagining them a flock of sheep. He mumbled while looking out of the window at children running and racing each other on the sidewalk, "forty heads." He wished he could be with the children and could share in their laughter.

"Is everyone here?" the driver asked in Spanish. "Except for two," the company representative answered in English. "Where are they?" David looked at the passengers then turned in despair to the driver. "I will go back to the airport and look for them." He wondered to himself, the passengers are bored, shall I tell them about my dream? Before he could get over his hesitation David returned to the bus running.

He got on the bus and closed the door behind him. "Where are they?" the driver asked, and the passengers stretched out their necks in anticipation. David muttered, "They got on another bus. It's not important. Let's move."

Act Two

He stood in front of the apartment door for a few minutes. It was on the third floor, on the roof of a new building. He was standing with his back to the horizon and the sea. He erased them from existence. He was looking at the key in his palm, trying to remember why he was there, and why he was carrying that key. "*Buenas tardes*, Señor." The cleaning lady going into the apartment next door drew him out of his reverie. He nodded in acknowledgement and went into his apartment in a hurry. He locked the door. He turned the key several times to make sure it was firmly locked.

He registered with his eyes the dimensions of the apartment. It was big. He would try to write down the measurements later. He would have to buy a measuring tape. There was a bedroom and a large bathroom. The kitchen opened out to the living room, which led to a balcony with a table and two chairs. An "X" made from black tape marked the glass door separating the living room from the balcony. He leaned on the balcony railing and looked down. He saw an uncovered swimming pool with a blue floor, right next to another swimming pool for children. His arm felt heavy, and he realized that he was still carrying his bag. He put it down on a side table. He must keep the place tidy. He thought, the room is too big for me, what will I do here, in this large room, why didn't she come with me, why did she make all the arrangements and send me away on my own, alone, so that she could stay with him? I know she wants to be with him, what about me?

A white apartment. The walls were white, the floor was white, and the plastic table and chairs were white. He walked around one more time looking for some color. Nothing. Only white. In different shades. He stood in the middle of the living room, finding pleasure in being where he thought was the heart of the apartment. If only he had a measuring tape to make sure of the distances and that where he was standing was the exact center of the place. He suddenly realized something very important was missing. He noticed the absence of a TV set. He felt a heavy sadness descend on his chest. What will I do in this big white place, why didn't she come with me? His eyes began to tear. If she had been with him she would have scolded him, and he would have said to her, hiding his tears, it is the sunlight coming through the big windows reflecting on the walls and on my eyes. For her sake, he covered his eyes with a pair of sunglasses and left the apartment.

Act Three

"We are ten minutes away from the beach." This was what the advertisement in the *Lanzarote Paradise* said. The reception office was closed. He wanted to borrow a measuring tape. 3 p.m. He left the building. The street was empty. The walls shielding the buildings on both sides of the street were constructed from stones. Most of them were black. Black walls. He walked slowly, enjoying the warm sunlight. He forced himself to slow down as he descended toward the sea. The houses here were painted white and blue. She loved white and blue. He would call her to tell her. No, no, not now. He remembered what his mother said to him. Call me in the evening. Rest first. Then organize your clothes. Call me after you have eaten.

A row of shops began to appear. Shops glorious with goods. Restaurants. Cafés. Ice-cream kiosks dotted the two sides of the road for tempting everyone going to the beach. He reached the beach. He looked at his watch. Exactly ten minutes. What the *Lanzarote Paradise* advertised was true then. The ground beneath his feet changed. He took off his shoes and walked on the beach, happy with the feel of the warm sand on his feet. He got closer and closer to the sea. He did not like getting his feet wet. He noticed how small the number of people taking walks on the beach was. He began counting them, one, two, ten . . . It was very difficult getting the count right.

Some were disturbed when they noticed his searching look. He too was disturbed by how disturbed they were. Too many of them. He had to get away. He tried to avoid tripping over their naked bodies. The sun was still warm in October.

He returned to the cement sidewalk, to the shops, most of which were open for business and window-shopping. Window-shopping more than sales. Colorful goods for all ages: the young and the old. In a shop he watched an old woman buy ten postcards. He bought ten of them too, just like her, five all black postcards with "Lanzarote at night" written on them, and five all white with "Lanzarote during the day" written on them. He put them in his pocket. He also bought, like her, five ashtrays made from the island's volcanic rocks.

He walked away from the tourist area. He withdrew from people. He walked on the volcanic rocks along a desolate landscape, inhaling the dry air free of insects. He gathered some stones and put them in his pocket. He sat on a high rock looking at the white birds flying around. He wanted them to come near him. He drew a square around them, framing them inside a TV screen his hand made, and absorbed himself in watching them. The seagulls were gliding in the air, soaring, how high were they going up?, and dropping, what was the distance separating him from them?, should he tell them about his dream? Alone on the isolated rock, before a screen his hands drew on the horizon, he felt the tremor of the night course through his body. He did not move from his place. He remained glued to the black rock, telling the seagulls flying away from the darkening Lanzarote beach what happened in his dream. He was saying . . .

Episode Two

Saint Ives, Britain, August 1999

9:10 p.m. My husband and I left the hotel in complete silence. Like two strangers, we avoided looking at each other. We walked along the external wall, through the front garden, and turned left onto a side street that ran parallel to the main street. I sighed loudly so as to attract his attention. It fell on deaf ears. He continued to look ahead, absorbed in his own thoughts, his eyes hidden behind the darkness of the side street and the edge of his hat. He loved rain, he said, and loved walking in the rain, but hated getting his hair wet. I sighed also because we left the hotel. We felt cheated when we were inside, imprisoned in our feeling of being cheated by Universe Tours Company.

When the bus brought us to the hotel, we saw right away a huge billboard standing in front advertising, "25 pounds per night," and realized we had paid the Universe Tours Company double. It was no use running from the bus to the hotel. Our light summer clothes got wet in the torrential rain. Who would have thought of wearing raincoats in August? The lady who owned the hotel laughed. "A stormy day, isn't it?" she said. "They mentioned in the news that we haven't seen the likes of it since 1968." "Would you like to have dinner or not," she asked us after registering our names. "No," I replied quickly, "thank you!"

In our very small, very tidy, dollhouse of a room, we found an electric kettle, a platter lined with bags of coffee, tea, sugar, and creamer. Two of each. Two glasses. Two mugs. My husband unpacked and neatly arranged his few clothes and belongings in the wardrobe. He always did this. "So that we can feel at home in the new place," he would say. This was precisely what I was afraid of, to leave my old place and start another journey of settling down in a new place, and I always left my clothes and things neatly packed in my suitcase, ready to return to my home. He asked me sharply, "Why did you say no to dinner?" "Because it is a small hotel and the dining room feels like a tomb," I said. "Isn't it better to have dinner in a restaurant overlooking the sea?" He looked to the window without interest, like a child being forced to look at something he has been refusing to see. The storm. The heavy rain beating the window glass. My illogical suggestion that we look for a restaurant overlooking the sea. What a start for a summer holiday meant to bring us closer. "Let's go out," he said.

We put out of our minds the storm, the tempestuous summer holiday, and the loss of a free dinner and walked to the nearest pub. We sat close to the bar. It was a small local pub that felt more like a simple living room in a house if it had not been for the bar standing in its left corner. The room was furnished with wood benches covered in colorful embroidered cushions. Everything was old except for the customers. The bar smelled normal, of smoke and alcohol, of different kinds of cigarettes and alcoholic drinks. The customers did not have their distinct odors. They seemed to have left them behind at the door when they closed their umbrellas. They shook them off and left them on the hangers outside before they came in.

The pub was divided into two sections, one for drinks only and another for dining. We sat in the drinks area. We wanted to eat but the waiter pointed to a big clock hanging on the wall and said very politely, "The kitchen closed a few minutes ago." He was a handsome young man who gave us his apology with a smile that lit up his face. "Our fault," we said in an understanding tone, "we came too late." "What do you have to drink?" my husband asked. "Beer." He ordered for himself a pint of beer and a shot of whiskey. I stole a look at the owner of the pub. A thin man wearing reading glasses so thick his eyes looked bigger than their normal size. The black frame reminded me of the reading glasses sold at charity shops and flea markets. Or maybe their owner died and his heir got rid of them. I said to my husband as he put a bag of roasted nuts in front of me, "I know a friend who kept his dead mother's dentures for years. He used to carry them wrapped in translucent tissue paper inside a red velvet pouch."

He said "to your health" and downed the shot of whiskey before he began sipping on his beer. "The waiter is wearing a dark blue shirt like Tony Blair," I said. "It must be the fashion," he said. "Do you think Che Guevara would have become the universal symbol for revolution and an icon for all generations if he had not been handsome?" "Why the question?"

"Our forgiving attitude toward the waiter and our acceptance of his abiding by the dining schedule to the second despite our abhorrence for all rituals of timekeeping." "Icons are not necessarily handsome." "For example?" "Ho Chi-minh." "Ho Chi-minh!" I screamed in protest, "But he was a handsome man. What if Che Guevara was a carbon copy of Idi Amin, for example?" "We can't build a theory on one example." "I know. But any theory begins with an observation. What about Castro?" He got up to fetch another beer.

At the bar he stood next to a man sitting on a high stool, looking at the barman, his assistant, and the shelves of bottles of alcohol behind them. He sat with his back to the crowd, to me. His body looked old, but his hair was jet black. Was it dyed? He was wearing a black shirt and a pair of black trousers with a line of red running from the waist to the foot on the side. I heard him tell my husband about seagulls. Gray seagulls were newly hatched chicks. White seagulls with bright red dots on their beaks were ready for mating. Seagulls were generally hateful to the fishermen because they stole their catch. And he stopped abruptly. My husband stood there, with a glass of beer in one hand and a shot of whiskey in another, waiting for him to add something new. But he had already turned his face away, now following the waiter's every move intently. The waiter, out of politeness, intervened, "and they attack each other viciously." My husband said, "Maybe that's how they survive." He waited for a few seconds for the young man to respond, but the young man was busy serving other customers. My husband turned around and came back to me.

I heard a voice in my head. It was the voice of our youngest son who had a mild case of autism. He would ask insistently, "Shall I tell you about my dream? Shall I tell you about my recurring dream?" I could still hear his voice ringing loudly in my head even when I was thousands of miles away. His voice. Shall I tell you about my dream? Shall I tell you about my dream? I held my head in my arms to silence the monotonous, piercing, and persistent voice. What was he doing now, far away, and at home all alone?

A young woman in her midtwenties sat next to us with a young man close in age. They came into the pub attached to each other like a pair of Siamese twins. They left again after a quick glass of beer still clinging to each other. The turnover was fast. We became a feature of the place after occupying the same space for longer than anyone else. We drank one glass after another with the seagull man, the waiter, and the owner of the pub.

Two young women occupied a neighboring bench. The owner of the pub spoke to one of them in a sharp tone when she complained about the brand of a bag of potato chips she was given and when she read out loud the expiry date. She also ordered two screwdrivers. She returned to her bench, sat down, and attached her body to her girlfriend.

My husband downed the third shot of whiskey with the third pint of beer. His face reddened and his voice began to shake. He advised me not to drink more than I could take so as not to disturb my stomach. We were now at the doorstop of the familiar place, I felt, and I wanted to avoid at all cost an inevitable fight. He would start an argument by asking, in profound bitterness, why do you care about him more than us? Why do you sacrifice our life for his sake? He is capable of living a reasonable life without you, so why do you insist on hanging on to him? Isn't he happier than us in his autism, in his estrangement from us and from the world? I could feel, as I replayed his arguments in my head, the worn-out tightrope I was walking on and that it would break off any minute. I must find a way to avert the ordeal of another hopeless argument and save our holiday from the tempests of our impossible problems.

I played the memory card and waved a key from the past. "This pub is small and cozy, just like the coffeehouses at home." Joy spread across his face as he caught the imaginary bait. "It reminds me of the coffeehouse my father used to take me to. Wood benches, mats, a stove covered in soot, thick black tea, 'Chai Noomi Basra,' with a glass of water. I also remember how my cousin Aziz got arrested in that coffeehouse. He went to prison during the 1956 revolution. All of them, my older brothers and cousins, went to prison in those days. Baghdad was raging with revolution." I sighed in relief. The distant past was the blanket that saved us from ourselves.

One of the young women returned to her girl-friend with two more screwdrivers and a bag of roasted nuts. The owner of the pub and the waiter looked at her in disgust. She sat, having put down the glasses on the small table in front of them, and held her friend in her arms again.

"Your cousin," I said, "why don't we record his memories and stories?" "The idea did occur to me, but he doesn't like tape recorders and would stutter or go completely quiet when he sees one." "Let's buy a small recorder and keep it hidden."

The young woman put her hand on her friend's hair and caressed it with affection. Her friend looked at her with eyes full of love.

"Everybody who heard his stories found them amazing." "I remember getting home one day after having taken part in the Suez demonstration. My father asked me, where's your younger brother, and when I said I don't know, he told me, go away and don't come back without him. I went back to the street. Demonstrators everywhere. I looked for my brother. I went to the Alfadl district (in old Baghdad). The police were everywhere too. I saw them chase a group of youth in the alleys. Women hid the demon-strators in their houses to protect them."

The young woman was crying silently. Her tears were falling on her cheeks. The other took out a yellow tissue from her handbag and wiped her friend's tears. The bell rang for the final drink of the night. The young woman got up quickly and made for the bar. My husband tripped on the leg of the table getting up to buy more beer. He fetched another pint.

"I saw Aziz giving a speech to a crowd. He demanded that the people unite and called for the formation of a united Arab army. That was a joke, wasn't it? Nobody understood what he was saying at the time. He was ahead of his time."

At that very moment my husband and I were close to each other, arm in arm at the floodgate of memory. The fire of bitterness went out, and the edge of our disagreement softened. He held my hand, and excitement shot through my body. I, too, had my own memories. I saw myself as a child sitting with my grandfather in a coffeehouse in Baghdad near al-Maydan Square. A cup of "Chai Noomi Basra" materialized before me. I did not drink it because I did not like it. My grandfather coaxed, "Try it, you will get used to it, you will like it." I could see in a far corner of the coffeehouse my husband, as he was now, speaking about his family, his neighborhood, and his memories. Aziz was giving a speech to a crowd. I was looking. I was listening. I would tell my mother later about what I had seen and heard. I could hear my grandmother scold my grandfather, "Shame, shame on you, little girls don't go to coffeehouses with men." What did my grandfather say? I did not hear his reply.

I heard the pub bell ring for the second and final times. I looked around me. The bench where the two young women sat was now empty. The dining area was in complete darkness. I picked up half words from what my husband was saying: "Aziz refuses to speak to a tape recorder, how do I talk him into it?" The young man was collecting empty glasses and ashtrays from the tables. He was reorganizing the benches and chairs. My husband staggered to get up, knocking his chair backward, and caused a great commotion in the empty pub. He walked to the door shouting joyously, "good . . . goodbye . . . goodbye." I followed him. At the door, I turned back and looked at the bar, looking for the bits of the present I had missed. I saw a black seagull with red spots glittering in the dark. He flapped his wings and whispered: "good . . . goodbye . . . goodbye."

Episode Three

Sicily, Italy, November 1999

Day One

The representative of the Universe Packaged Tours Company met us with a welcoming smile. "How many are you?" she asked. "Two." She said, her voice full of disappointment, "I thought you were six." "No, only two." We followed her to the bus that would take us to our hotel, in Taormina, a hilltop town on the east coast of Sicily. We were the first to arrive at the bus because we had little luggage. I had advised my youngest son to do this when I arranged his first trip alone to Lanzarote. The other passengers were still waiting for their bags.

I sat on the bus while he took a stroll. He wanted to look at the new place. It was crowded with German and English tourists dragging heavy suitcases by their leather belts as if they were pulling their dogs by the leashes. Groups and individuals were hurrying out of the airport toward the buses numbered according to their holiday destination. I remained in my seat and watched people from the window for a few minutes. The sun was shining. The air in the bus was as stifling as a greenhouse. I got out of the bus and stood under a tree a few meters away. I did not take a walk or go far. I was afraid the bus would leave without me and I would be lost and alone. That was one of my fears. What if the driver changed his mind and drove away while I was taking a walk in the car park? What guarantees did I have that I would find another means of transportation?

The passengers were arriving at the bus. Big suitcases. Small suitcases. Hats. Winter coats. Summer jackets. Prepared for all kinds of weather. Gloomy faces we used to see in London, stubbornly harsh, turned away from others, or buried in the pages of newspapers or books, took off their masks as soon as they arrived at this holiday destination. Their faces rosy from the excitement of the journey and from the promise of a restful holiday: sunbathing, relaxing, stretching out on a beach, making love, and eating delicious food.

I went back to the bus. Another fear gripped me. What if someone decided to take my seat? I had the same anxiety attack every time I arrived at the airport. I had to be the first to board as if I needed to in order to get a window seat. I got up as soon as the plane landed and pushed through the passengers crowded in the narrow passageway to be the first to get through passport control and customs. I had to be the first to greet the company representative.

I sighed aloud, looking out of the window. When will my son come back? Where did he go? The driver may close the door and drive off. I pressed my face against the window. I followed the driver's every move. He was helping passengers loading their suitcases onto the luggage bay. Some passengers were joking with him in the few Italian words they knew. Suddenly, I heard, "Come here, come on, put it here, let him carry it for you, don't break your back." What a surprise, someone was speaking Arabic in the Iraqi dialect. An Iraqi reunion in Sicily! I was reminded of the song, "Gracious may the one be who brought us together without appointment." I saw a woman in her late forties with short black hair. Dyed for sure. The wrinkles on her face demanded white hair. And a dark-skinned man who looked a lot like the woman but for the dyed hair. His hair was gray and framed his round bald spot on the back of his head. He had a big nose, an upside down cup, sitting on the lower part of his face. A man and a woman came after them. They had Iraqi features too. They came in a group.

I could not hear the rest of what they were saying. My son had returned, and I was busy asking him about what he had seen and what was worth seeing in a huge car park and in such heat and humidity. He did not answer me. He could sense my nervousness and I shut up. "We have Iraqis with us," I said. "Really? How do you know?" "I heard one of them speak in pure Baghdadi." "I will check their passports," he teased, "as soon as they get on the bus." They got on one after another with the rest of the passengers. They saw my big smile, ignored me, and walked past in a hurry, avoiding the empty seats nearby, and chose to sit at the back of the bus. "They are strange," I whispered in his ear, "they didn't smile." He said loudly, "Why are you whispering? Speak normal!" "I don't want them to hear me." "Who says they are Iraqis? Maybe they don't want to talk to strangers. They are on holiday and it's their right."

Day Two

I said "Good Morning!" in Arabic to the woman with dyed hair. She pretended not to hear me. She looked to the members of her group some distance away, hoping they would come to her rescue. She then fixed her sight on food. She put two boiled eggs, a large piece of white cheese, slices of tomato, and some black olives on her plate. We were sitting in the hotel restaurant overlooking the sea on one side and the mountain on the other, having breakfast from the wonderfully generous and beautifully presented buffet. "You won't believe what happened. I said good morning to the Iraqi woman and she didn't answer me." He said in a tired voice, "Who says she is Iraqi?" "If you saw what she had chosen to eat for her breakfast, you would know right away she is Iraqi." "Mama, please leave those people alone. Maybe she didn't understand your murmurs and didn't want to embarrass you."

Day Three

I looked around the restaurant when we were at the dinner party. Sicilian music was playing in the background. I got up four times to refill my plate with different kinds of food from the buffet. Soup followed by appetizers, then grilled fish with roast potatoes and finally Dondurma ice cream. I intentionally walked by the table of four Iraqis every time I went back for more food. I did not hear the Iraqi dialect again. I said to him, "They lowered their voices every time I passed by." "Mama, if I can't hear what you're saying, and I'm sitting right next to you, because the music is so loud, how can they, especially when you're creeping around like a spy?"

Day Four

I did not run into them at the buffet, not in the morning at breakfast, nor in the evening at dinner. Maybe they had gone to Siracusa on the advertised company tour. Or maybe they had their lunch in the hotel and made do with it, unlike us; our package included only breakfast and dinner.

Day Five

My son and I got on the slow elevator taking us from the reception hall to our rooms in the hotel (the hotel was built into, or rather, carved into the mountain) at the same time as two members of the group. The woman, in her fifties, was short and fat, but had pleasant facial features. I thought she looked like a traditional Iraqi mother. I said good evening in English and they replied good evening in English with a very strong accent. I looked at my son sheepishly. I wanted to let him know, what did I tell you, they are Iraqis! They were absorbed in a conversation in Italian. He pointed up at the mountain, then down at the sea, and they exchanged a few sentences. The woman pointed at flowers on the mountain slope that brushed against the glass wall every time the elevator went down, and they exchanged a smile. They seemed to be sharing a secret about flowers.

On a deserted beach we sat on the bottom of a canoe parked upside down. Only a few seagulls were there, looking for food remains. "It is the end of the holiday season," my son said, pointing at the seagulls. He wanted to say something but changed his mind. I played with the pebbles around my trainers, feeling very close to him. I wanted to tell him how happy I was having him with me, even for just a few days. I was with him free of housework and away from his father and younger brother. What a difference between the two brothers! The other was clingy, like a sickness, and only brute force could drag him away from me. His look reminded me that he did not like to talk about his feelings. "The woman in the elevator," I said, "looks Iraqi, don't you think?" "Mama, please, God give you a long life, I beg you, let's talk about something else. What do you think of the sea, for example?" "Beautiful, but, did you notice how they were speaking Italian so slowly, not like other Italians?" In spite of himself, he got dragged into the conversation. "It's how they speak. People speak differently." "I have a new theory. What do you think? They are Iraqis who lived in Italy for some time then moved to Britain and now they are back for a visit." He did not answer. He walked toward the water in deliberate, slow steps, and stopped at the uprush of waves, then moved forward at the backwash, stopped again at the next uprush, and got closer to the sea yet again at the following backwash.

Day Six

We were late getting to the day tour bus. The English tour guide rebuked us. "You're late! It's past eight o'clock." My son replied in a sharp tone that was uncharacteristic of him and at odds with his usual polite treatment of workers in the service sector. "That damned elevator. There were tens of people waiting in line." I said to him, "You are just like Susan." He turned his face away. He pretended to look at our fellow passengers getting on the bus, then taking the front-row seats. After a short while, he said teasingly, trying to change the familiar subject of his wife, "Where are your Iraqi friends?" I smiled and whispered, "I saw the four of them in the front row of the lower deck." He whispered, imitating me, "𒀀𒌅𒆷 𒀀𒁲 𒈾 𒌋𒅗𒊏𒈨 𒉺𒀀𒈨𒋛 𒂍𒇲𒄩𒀀 𒅆𒈾𒉺𒋛 𒈨𒌋𒇲𒌈." "I know, I know, I can read your cards, you want to shut me up with one of your ancient texts. What is it this time?" "The first two lines from a Babylonian poem about creation in the Akkadian language." "What do they mean, if you don't mind explaining them to me, please, and what does it have to do with my reply?" "I don't really know, but I thought of them as soon as you mentioned the word 'lower.' Here's the translation: 'When on high the heavens had not been called (into being) / Below the earth had not been fashioned with a name.'" The tour guide raised her voice to name the villages and neighborhoods we passed on our way to one of the volcanoes on Mount Etna. "This is Zafferana, the village the lava almost drowned in 1992."

My son only agreed to come on this day trip organized by Universe after many heated discussions. He refused to go on any trip with the English. "Isn't it enough that I live with them day and night?" he said. I said, in spite of myself, "You could have chosen to live with them during the day only." He went quiet, as he usually did in recent months, since he moved back with us, having separated from his wife, Susan, and while waiting for his divorce to come through. Silence was his way of avoiding conflict. It was his answer.

I regretted what I said right away. I felt the cruelty of my cold words. My eyes teared up. I looked through the translucent curtain of my tears at his youthful face. The years may not leave traces on his face but will dig deep furrows into his heart. I felt the need to touch him. I put my hand on his hand and squeezed it affectionately. I felt him withdraw.

He pulled his hand away quickly. He added jokingly, "The gods may help you to find out who the people sitting in the lower deck are today."

Day Seven

We packed our bags and left for the restaurant to have our last breakfast before leaving for the airport in the company bus. He said, sipping with great pleasure a glass of juice, "When the tour guide told us about the bitter Sicilian orange juice and their failure to market it because it needed too much sugar for it to be drinkable, I had no idea she meant our Narange." "Your grandfather used to squeeze Narange and add a lot of sugar to it for us to drink as juice." "I remember that. When was the last time we drank Narange juice?" "1974? Thereabouts. I don't remember exactly." Silence. "Did you notice how they avoided us all day yesterday?" "Who?" "The Four Musketeers." "Yes. I don't see them today. They must have bought a two-week holiday. They will stay another week." I drank my Narange juice very slowly, sip by sip, wanting to keep its familiar taste forever. I wanted the intimacy to last an eternity. "Too much sugar in the juice," I said. "Your grandfather got the balance just right." He did not answer. He nodded his head in agreement.

Episode Four

Ireland, Train from Dublin to West Point, August 2000

Scene One

He handed me a sandwich in Saran wrap. I thought he was inviting me to share in his lunch. "Thank you very much," I said to him quickly, "I'm not hungry." He said, "Unwrap it." I smiled apologetically, peeled off the transparent wrap for him, and he thanked me. He said, "My fingers are useless as you can see." He showed me his twisted fingers. And like a child showing off, he let me see them a second time. "They were sawed off when I was injured. They got infected and they cut them off." He pointed with his head at a woman sleeping next to him. "She was beside me. I told the surgical team that I wouldn't let them operate if she couldn't be with me. They protested but I insisted and eventually they gave in. They put her in a sanitized surgical gown and she stayed close." He laughed, happy with his triumph over the doctors, hospital administration, and infection. "My motto in life, as you see," he said loudly, "is 'persist right or wrong and you'll get what you want.' 'Accepting reality' does not exist in my vocabulary." He laughed through his blackened loose teeth. "It is true, we all believe in this." "All?" I wondered. "Yes," he said, "in Ireland."

I had a forward-facing window seat. I booked the trip through Universe Tours Company, which my wife liked to use—she insisted that it offered the best packages for holidays inside and outside Britain. The Irishman and his wife, who seemed in their sixties, were sitting facing me. The woman was wearing a white dress with red and blue flowers under a cardigan with horizontal stripes. She was asleep, and that was why I looked in her direction when I looked up from my book every now and then. I avoided exchanging looks with strangers. I did notice the brown, gray, and blond streaks of her hair, for my wife wore a similar cocktail on her head. She was clutching her black handbag to her bosom on top of a *Daily Express* newspaper on her lap. A small suitcase sat between her legs on the ground. It was a gift from Barclay's Bank. "Barclays: the bank that listens to you" was written on it in bold letters. "Where are you from?" he asked.

The question slapped me in the face. The unspeakable was happening again. I swallowed hard. I took time to answer. I was, to be honest, pretty fed up with strangers throwing the same question at me, and so freely, everywhere I went. Also, I did not go on a trip on my own, alone, so as to find myself chatting with a person who raised his voice on the train, laughing proudly about his severed fingers and attracting attention to himself. And I really preferred silence when I was on holiday—I just wanted to look around.

"Iraq," I said, adding very quickly, "but I live in London." I was trying to avoid the usual comments or questions that would come after the initial bait. There would be nothing new. It would be a routine conversation, as boring as the routines of a hospital patient, that would go like this: "From Iran?" "No, Iraq." "Iraq?" "Yes, the country whose name ends in a *q* not an *n*. Iraq is a neighboring country of Iran." "Oh, I see, you mean Khomeini's country!" "No, it's a country owned by nobody from what I know, its president is called . . ." Stop, don't say anything, Iraq is Saddam's country, isn't it?

But the old Irishman would not have any of it. He stopped chewing and said sadly, "I'm so sorry for the Iraqi people. They are going through tough times. Just like us in Ireland." I was surprised. Who was it that said, "There is nothing surprising anymore," and he chose death. I was meeting a man who could sum up everything he wanted to say in two sentences. He knew, and that was amazing. I did not have to explain. He stretched out his hand with severed fingers to shake mine. "My name is Brian," nodding his head at his wife, "and she's Mary."

"You haven't been to St. Patrick?" Brian was incredulous. "You've been in Ireland for days and you haven't been to see St. Patrick?" "I don't believe in visiting saints' tombs," I said apologetically. He gave out his loud, affectionate laugh. "You will believe, you will. We all started like that when we were young.

Wait till you get to be my age, and live with a woman like her," he said in a conspiratorial tone while looking at his wife, "you will believe. St. Patrick is no ordinary saint. He is more than a saint. Haven't you noticed that there are no snakes in Ireland?" I said, apologetically again, "My itinerary was organized by Universe, and it did not include St. Patrick." "How on earth could you let a despicable tourist company stop you from visiting St. Patrick?" He shouted in anger, "Fuck Universe!"

Scene Two

Brian and Mary insisted on buying me a beer at a pub near the train station. "Just one pint," they said in unison, "to wash off our fatigue from the journey." Brian said, "This is an excellent pub only the locals know about. Come, you must try the true Irish Guinness! Once you've tasted it, I promise you, you'll realize that what they sell you in London is black water." We stayed in the pub for hours longer than the train journey. We stopped counting after the third beer. I did not remember what we said, but I remembered Mary's beautiful voice as she stood in the middle of the pub and sang with us singing along. As we said goodbye at the pub door, Brian lifted his glass high and shouted with all his might, "Iraq," and I lifted my glass, which felt so heavy by then, and tried to imitate his cheer, "Ireland!" I hugged them, crying. I promised them through the tears running down my face that I would change my itinerary and make sure to visit St. Patrick.

Scene Three

A huge crowd was gathering around the Down Cathedral on the drumlins of Downpatrick. Children, young men and women, and old people leaning on their walking sticks arrived in private cars, public buses, or tour buses. The sun was out, basking our bodies in its warmth. An old man standing next to me, noticing my confusion, asked, "Is this your first pilgrimage?" "Yes," I answered. "Better rent a walking stick from the shop and bring a bottle of water with you. The path up Cathedral Hills to St. Patrick's Grave is long and steep."

I lifted my head high but could not see the mountaintop. I saw instead small shapes that looked like ants crawling up the slopes. My heart sank. I realized the grave mistake I had made in coming here. What was I doing on this silly tour, having committed myself to being herded like a sheep in a flock? I would have done better walking around in the city, sitting in a pub or a café, reading newspapers and writing a postcard to my wife and son. I was feeling stuck. I remembered my promise to Brian and Mary, sighed, and joined the moving crowd.

I convinced myself that St. Patrick would be the first of God's munificent friends I visited willingly, or fulfilling friends' wishes. I had made pilgrimages to shrines with my family during holy seasons, or even on a normal day, in which I had no say as a child and teenager, but which I abandoned without a backward glance in my youth. Kazim, Karbala, Najaf Imams, and 'Abd al-Qadir al-Gilani. How many prayers did my mother say while she hung on to the windows of their tombs! She prayed for Iraq's prosperity, and my sister's health, wishing her to marry a good boy from a good family as soon as possible. She got the exact opposite of what she prayed for. I had been in exile for twenty years, and my sister in Baghdad was a confirmed spinster. Thankfully my mother did not live long enough to see the effect of her prayers on Iraq.

I was pleased I had put on a pair of good sports shoes. They "protected the feet and prevented slipping," as my youngest son would say, defending his choice of wearing sports shoes all the time. Or did I hear this in a TV ad? I could not remember. I noticed that the old man walking, or rather crawling behind me with the help of a cane, was wearing a pair of strange-looking shoes. I had never seen the likes before. Perhaps they were custom-made for him. The old man smiled at me. "I see that you didn't take my advice! You may be right. Young people don't need walking sticks." I decided to walk a bit faster to avoid going into another maze of meaningless chitchat.

It was not easy to get away though, for the ground beneath my feet changed from aged asphalt to rocky terrains covered in sand that was in turn covered with fine pebbles. Every step taken without careful calculation would surely lead to slipping and falling on one's face. We began our ascent from sea level. I looked back once we reached a reasonable height and saw a beautiful scene of nature taking shape before my eyes: rolling green hills reaching all the way to the sea. I could hear water rippling and dogs barking. I read in the travel guide that the mountain was 800 meters tall. The size of the rocks grew bigger as we climbed higher. They looked like pebbles at first. When I looked closely I realized they were stones of different shape and size. The layer of earth covering them was light, like the fuzz growing on a teenage boy's face. The mountain had a teenager's fuzz! A layer of sand was sprinkled over the rocks to disguise their ruggedness. Above us in a distance, I saw a flock of sheep, and further up, on the rugged rocks, a drove of goats. The mountain smelled of droppings and dung. He was one of God's munificent friends, I thought to myself, who loved to live in nature's arms. He was at one with nature. He was a green saint. I laughed, in spite of myself, and loudly too, but I quickly stifled my laugh. I looked around, expecting to hear my mother's voice, scolding me, don't laugh when you're visiting with the saints, it's prohibited, *Haram.*

I stopped and stood with the others before a small statue of a woman holding a child in her arms. The woman was of course Mary and the child Jesus. A small basin lay at her feet. The old man, appearing out of nowhere, stood beside me. "Dip your hand in the water, then wipe your forehead." I immediately did what the old man said, cursing Brian under my breath for getting me into this jam. I also cursed my own cowardice, which made me respect old people and obey them even when they went senile. Why didn't I scream in his face and say no? I did as I was told. This was the last time I listened to anyone. My oldest son would never have done anything he was told without checking and double-checking with tens of questions, of how do you prove what you claim?, and I, I obeyed an old man I did not even know just like that. Damn Brian, damn Mary, damn St. Pat . . . I slipped and fell on my face. Hot liquid streaked down my nose. My eyes were stinging with pain. Scratches covered my arms and legs. The old man helped me up and gave me a white handkerchief smelling of carnation and incense. "Watch your step," he said calmly, "we've only just started." I looked at my watch. 12:10 p.m. We had two more hours of climbing ahead of us. I focused on my steps. I avoided small stones and walked on big stones, bending my body forward in search of a center of gravity. My leg muscles were not used to this kind of slow climb, and they complained of the ache and from the pain of the scratches on them.

A young woman walked past me, dragging behind her three children tied to leashes that held them from falling. They were laughing. She seemed to have been able to make it fun for them. She convinced them that they were playing a game with certain rules. The children stood enthusiastically in front of a medium-sized stone statue of the Christ protected by a low metal fence. The young woman said, "This is the second stage of our pilgrimage. Go around the statue seven times and repeat 'Hail Mary' seven times." The children ran around the statue counting aloud, one, two, three, four, five, six, and seven. "Seven more times," she said, "and now say 'Hail Jesus' seven times." She hugged and kissed each of them as they completed their run. I watched the children sitting on a rock nearby. Where was the mountaintop? We were still going up. The young woman and her children were now quite a distance ahead of me, and I could no longer make out the bent back of the old man. All of a sudden I was seeing a completely different scene. I saw a line on the plain before me formed by the winding caravan of pilgrims connecting the next mountain with where I sat watching, a rocky corridor where pilgrims caught their breath momentarily before they embarked on their second climb.

The next mountain, a composite of craggy rocks, looked more like an eight in a child's drawing. Red earth covered the corridor between the two mountains. It was wet. We were even more likely to lose our balance. The hot sunlight was slapping my face, and I felt a sudden thirst. Out of nowhere a cloud of insects raided us. The pilgrims waved at them, trying to get them away from their faces, exposed arms, and legs sticking out of their shorts. Fortunately I still felt the awe of holy places in me and thought shorts inappropriate for visiting saints, even if they had been sleeping on a mountaintop for hundreds of years. If my mother could see me now, I thought, respecting customs and traditions I would not accept before, not even for her sake, she would have been proud. An old woman ahead of me slipped, and I instinctively put my hand on her back to hold her steady. I sat her down on a rock nearby. She said in jest, "I don't know why I'm in such a hurry. I'm sure St. Patrick will wait for me. I'll rest a bit then continue climbing."

The protruding edges of the rocks were sharp and could cut. Some were like thorns sticking out of stems and roots invisibly buried in the mountain. Others were like shells or skins that fell apart as soon as we put our hands on them. We were climbing on all fours now. There were no railings, fences, or footholds for climbers to lean on. I climbed with the rest of the pilgrims. Our feet searched for footholds. We bent our bodies to keep our balance. Our faces reddened. Our exhausted bodies were perspiring profusely. Our shirts and sweaters were soaking wet. We were struggling for air. Everybody was overwhelmed by the same feeling of one in all and all in one. We were a part of the mountain. The mountain was a part of nature. Where was the Saint's Grave in this sea of unity? We must be getting very close to the top, to the Grave. We could see the faces of the descending crowd shine with happiness. They greeted us enthusiastically and encouraged us to continue climbing when they saw that some of us were about to give up from exhaustion. "Just a few more steps, it's a short distance away." "Go, go on, it is a terrific experience."

My joints and muscles were in pain, and the insect bites on my face were swelling up. I felt a sudden rush of air push me from behind and turned very cold. Did the temperature drop? Did the air pick up speed? Or was I coming down with a cold? We were only a few meters away from the Grave. Everybody was speeding up, driven by their longing and impatience. The old recovered their energy, and the young were promised new games. St. Patrick, here we are, St. Patrick, come to see you. "A few more steps and we'll be there," my mother held my hand firmly in hers so that I would not get lost and coaxed me to continue walking with her. "Mama," I pleaded, "Mama, I'm very tired." "We will visit the Imam first," she answered me patiently, "and then we will rest. You'll see for yourself how good you'll feel." We were circumambulating around the fenced-in tomb in a large circle formed by human bodies, being carried forward by the legs of the crowd. I could hear our guide recite in a strong quiet voice: "Peace be upon the chosen friends of God. Peace be upon the allies of Abu 'Abdallah. Love to our Prophet and blessings on our Imam. Blessings on the earth where you lie. May we share in your victory!"

I felt exhausted. This body in its fifties let me down. How did I manage to remember the words of a prayer from so distant a past when I could not even remember a sentence, a number, or a name? My weakened body was telling me to turn around, to give up, but the energy of the ascending bodies carried me up. I found refuge in them and let go of my control. Up and up we went. The cool breeze dried our sweat. Our faces brightened. The urgency of doubt and protest calmed down. I gave in and gradually the heaviness of my spirit lifted. Even my body became light. I was reaching the top and the cool shaded area. I looked up. The face of the old man peered down at me from the edge of the mountaintop, his friendly eyes, his silver hair, his smell of incense and all, smiling and encouraging. He was looking straight in my eye, and I saw in the clarity of his eyes the reflection of his face in my own eyes. I tripped. He reached out to me with his hand and pulled me toward him.

Episode Five

Álora, Spain, April 2001

I ran away from Fuengirola, from the packaged holiday organized by Universe, and from the hotel jam-packed with tourists. From the coastal town filled with the smell of fish and chips, the noise the children on spring holiday made, the uniform gift items displayed in shops, the instructive pictures of local dishes restaurants pasted on the walls, and from pizza, hamburger, and banana and strawberry milkshakes. I remembered my friend, Brian, and what he said, "Why on earth do you allow a despicable company to arrange your life?" The company, my wife, how I lived my life, I've had it, all of it. In a moment of lucidity, I decided it was the last time I let this happen to me. I took the first train from Fuengirola to Málaga, and from Málaga to the end of the line.

"Álora is the last stop on the line," the conductor said, when he noticed my hesitation getting off. I was the last to disembark. I exited the train station that was more like a cozy, neat, family living room, and stood on the sidewalk looking around. Where did everyone disappear to? The sky was blue and the sun was warm. I could feel her rays coming through my cotton shirt and trousers. How I missed the sun, her light and warmth! The road on my right looked as if it would descend into a flat plain. I saw the one on my left go uphill and took it. The empty road was fenced in from the side overlooking a valley. I walked fast, and a few minutes later the road began to wind around and up the mountain, which reminded me of the steep path up to Saladin summer resort and of the Spiral Minaret in Samarra. I looked for the street name. Nothing. I could see small houses built on the right side of the road with tiny windows that looked like openings of mountain caves. Álora was one of the municipalities of al-Andalus. Why was the architecture here so different? The row of houses grew in number. Did the houses sweat under the warm sun? I saw an open door. I pretended to amble along, stealing looks through the door, hoping to find an Andalusian courtyard with a fountain surrounded by beautiful plants in the middle. Nothing. I caught a glimpse of a small living room in semidarkness. No plants. No people.

Like a tree sprouting too many branches, the road forked into innumerable alleys. I stopped for a moment, then continued on to the right. I looked up and a sign reading "Alley of Anxious Hearts" appeared suddenly in my view; so did a Black man carrying a jug in one hand and a cane in the other and a sack on his back. "Peace be upon you!" he greeted me, and I replied, "Peace be upon you, and the mercy and blessings of God!" "Who are you?" he asked in Persian. I said, "Someone who lost his way," and he said, "So am I." He fetched water in his jug. I wanted to drink. He said, "Be patient!" then opened his sack and brought out a handful of roast chickpeas and rice. I ate and drank. He asked me about my name.

"Muhammad," I said, and asked him about his. "al-Qalb al-Fāriḥ," he said to me in Arabic, "Rejoicing Heart."

Steady climb. Up and up I went. Breathless steps. Fast beating heart. Hair and beard moist with sweat. Sweat running down my spine and the back of my legs. I must have chosen the wrong path. Didn't anybody live here? I almost went back the same way I came when I reached the end of the path, only to realize at the last minute that it opened out to a spacious square that revived the soul and refreshed the eye. It was the town center and her heart. A church with a steeple and a bell stood in the middle. It was accessible by stone steps that raised it up above human preoccupations. A drunk was sleeping on one of the steps. He looked like a statue. His skin was the same color as the stone step he lay on. The place smelled of dust and droppings of pigeons sheltering in the cavities of the various shapes decorating the church exterior. The drunk, holding a bottle of wine in his arms, was looking ahead absentmindedly with half-closed eyes.

I sat on a wood bench facing the church and the drunk, watching three boys and a girl playing on an ancient tree, climbing up and coming down. The church was closed. The shops on the square were closed. Álora was taking a siesta. None of the children looked at me, unlike other village children, who ran behind strangers, shouting and clapping their hands. What happened to Álora's children? After a short break, when my heartbeat slowed to a normal pace, I set out on a narrow path marked by a street sign that said "Way to the Castle." Up I went again. Up and up until I reached a walled-in dirt square below the castle with a few benches sparsely placed around its corners, each offering a different view. One could sit and enjoy looking at the expansive horizon above, or the foot of the mountain on the right, or the town center built on the waist of the mountain on the left, or the plains colorful with trees, the wide river, and the distant villages ahead.

I stopped in front of the castle wall. I focused on the section on my right, at the three modern texts written in Spanish next to a scene painted on the wall. It was of an Arab man on a horse carrying a young girl wearing a white dentelle dress in front of him. He was holding the girl with his right arm and fending off the spears pointed at them with his left arm. The soldiers were many, and the spears were drawn. The girl's face shrank in fear, and the man's bearded face twisted with anger and bitterness. His clothes were simple. Was he the last defender of the castle and one of the last to leave Álora, al-Andalus, the country, life?

I walked up five steps. I reached the castle gate at the top of the worn-out stone steps. Above it I read the faint traces of this phrase in Arabic, "The way of Allah is our only guide. The gate of Allah is our only way." On my right, I saw a well-worn prayer room furnished with some benches. The statue of a veiled

bald woman stood in the prayer niche. She was holding in her arms a baby gazing at the halo around her
head. "It is a monastery revered by the Christians,"
Ibn Battutah reported in his travelogue. "One of its
walls rose a hundred feet into the sky. Many priests
and peasants lived there. *Tales of the Prophets* were
carved into the walls. The altar inside had a marble
floor on which feet slid and slipped. The statue of
Mary standing against the wall had her eye on you
whichever way you turned your head. It had a guest-
house that provided accommodation and hospitality
for the passers-by." A wall built from stones laid in
horizontal courses surrounded the uncovered courtyard. It had eight towers, four on the four corners,
and one in the middle of each of the four stretches.
A tall balcony stood in the middle of the courtyard.
The prince, or commander, could sit on it and keep
watch of his dominion from all sides as well as of
those entering the castle.

These walls were lined with the dead, who looked
over the comings and goings through glass windows
framed by marble with their names, dates, and places
of death carved into it. Children. Babies. Men. And
women. I caught glimpses of their lives on some of
the faint portraits on their coffins. All the portraits
were yellow regardless of the age or time of death,
as if entering the world of the dead required them to
show photos of specific requirements from which the
colors of life receded. The dead were built into the
walls. They were the bricks of the castle. Hundreds.

Thousands. The walls became too crowded. Extensions were built. Imaginary walls were built, rising high like murals, or mobile library shelves. Every dead body was offered custom-made flowers placed outside their windows to bloom forever.

More worn-out steps took me to the next level of the castle, to another dirt square. A lone fruitless fig tree stood in the middle surrounded on four sides by lemon trees heavy with fruits unpicked from the previous season, side by side with this season's blossoms. I looked around before I picked two lemons and a few flowers. I brought them close to my nose and inhaled deeply, but they had no smell, none of the perfume of citrus blossoms I knew, or the refreshing scent of lemons.

I realized suddenly that the air was still and the place was quiet with a silence that scratched the senses. There was no life. I was frightened. I wanted to escape. I rushed down the steps, taking them two at a time. At the castle gate, a child in a white dentelle dress caught my attention, and I stopped for a brief moment. I threw the lemons and the flowers into her hands stretched out toward me as if to stop me from my course. I could see a smile spread across her waxy face.

Episode Six

Family Home, London, July 2002

In the kitchen the water in the electric kettle was about to boil. The sound of simmering water was rising gradually, from faint murmurs to loud whispers then to a racket that filled up the whole place. This musical fight among the small particles that spun around the room was accompanied by the goldfinch chirping, like a child, a familiar tune, "Mādhā? What?" He was hopping in the cage, from one corner to another. As the noise of the kettle rose, he sang his different tunes, louder and faster, raising the volume higher and higher, and extending his breaths longer and longer. The water boiled, electricity cut off automatically, and the goldfinch stopped singing.

"You have to return him to his owners."

"I know."

"When?"

"Tomorrow. Thursday."

"But you have been saying tomorrow for two weeks," he laughed, mocking.

"I know."

"When will you take him back to them then?"

"Tomorrow."

The feathers of the goldfinch were colorful. His head was gray with a tinge of yellow. It reminded her of her younger brother whose hair turned white when he was ten. The children of the alley used to run after him and chant, "Old man, old man with white hair,

141

old man." A bit of black had crept into the tip of the goldfinch's wings too. When he flapped his wings and flew, he created a vision of beautiful colors, which she enjoyed watching.

"He is beautiful."

"I know."

"Let's open the door for him. What do you think?"

"No," she replied sharply.

"Why not?"

"Because he will fly away and never come back. If he goes far away he will die."

"He will learn how to live outside."

"No. He was born in a cage. He does not know how to live outside. He will die."

"He will at least have a chance to fly. Instead of jumping like a frog."

"He will die."

"He will die soaring with his wings."

"Death is death."

She brought out a fig for him. She stuck it to the wires of the cage wall next to a lettuce leaf. She lined the bottom with a new sheet from an Arabic newspaper. She read the headlines aloud to the goldfinch: "Minibus drivers cross the streets of Beirut in protest." The news occupied the bottom third of the page. "65 members of the Jamaa Islamiyya in Egyptian prisons protest against their leaders." In the folded corner of the newspaper page, she read, "Agreement between Barazani and Talebani ends electricity supply problems in Kurdistan." She asked the goldfinch, "Did you hear?"

The silent goldfinch dozed off, puffing up his feather and hiding his head between his wings. He looked like a colorful ball.

"Look at the way he is jumping in his small cage."

"I know. He is energetic."

"He wants to fly."

"No. Nightingales are kept in cages alone except when they are mating."

"But he wants to fly. Look at him. Can't you see how he raises his wings, then lowers them in defeat?"

"He moves around enough," she answered him in stubbornness.

"Let's move his cage to the garden, for just a short while? What do you think?"

"Why? He is happy here."

"So that he can get some clean fresh air, to get to know another place outside the kitchen?"

"No."

"Why not?"

"Because . . . He will get cold. He is happy here, in the kitchen."

"If he is happy, why isn't he singing?"

"Because I haven't turned on the washer yet."

The goldfinch puffed up, jumped from one corner to another, flapped his wings halfheartedly, then lowered his head, picked up some nuts followed by some grains of sand placed in a small bowl to help with his digestion. She looked at him affectionately as she dragged the laundry basket out and sorted through the dirty clothes. She left the colors inside the basket and put the whites in the washer. She said to the gold-finch: "Once, Hassoun, my little one, I put the white clothes in the washer with a pair of red socks without noticing. The result was a catastrophe. All the clothes turned pink." She put her head very close to the cage, "His underwear," she said wickedly, "turned pink, like girls." She laughed out loud at her own joke, and the goldfinch jumped to the other side of the cage.

She pressed a button on the washer. There were tens of cycles but she used only one and always at 40 degrees. The drum began turning, slowly first, then picking up speed until it reached a thousand spins. The goldfinch cooed, letting out a sharp sound as he stood still in his place. He stopped jumping. He began chirping in different scales as if competing with the machine. He was very still. Nothing moved but the yellow fuzz on his throat. She brought a wood chair and sat facing him, listening to him releasing his voice from prison. She read once that the voices of birds were like their colors, camouflage, but why would a prisoner put on camouflage?

"If he had been created for jumping alone, why would he need two wings?"

"I know."

"Why do you keep him in a prison, then, in a cage? This is imprisonment."

"No."

"Give him back to his owners. They have a bigger cage and he'll have friends."

She felt a great pain squeeze her heart, and answered him sharply, "Tomorrow."

"Tomorrow, tomorrow, what? Thursday, Wednesday, Tuesday, tomorrow, yesterday, or last week?"

She grabbed a broom and swept the floor around the cage, collecting nutshells and feathers. She worked, all the while cooing at the goldfinch, "Hassoun, Hassoun." She had to cook. What should she make? She did not get a chance to ask him. He left in anger. She felt tired and sat on a chair. The wash cycle would end soon, and she would have to hang the clothes on the rope in the garden, collect them, iron them, fold them, and arrange them in the wardrobe. Why did he get angry this morning? She did not remember. Because of the goldfinch? Or what? They no longer needed an excuse to fight. He got angry, slammed the door behind him, and walked out, leaving her to sit in front of the goldfinch. Did he ask her, "When will you return him to his owners?" She did not remember. Perhaps. When would she return him to his owners? Tomorrow. She took a deep breath. Hassoun, O, Hassoun, when tomorrow? She had to hang the clothes first, cook, iron, clean the house, go shopping, go, shop, when, tomorrow?

Haifa Zangana was an advisor for the United Nations Development Programme report *Towards the Rise of Women in the Arab World* (2005). As a consultant for the United Nations Economic and Social Commission for Western Asia, she contributed to the *Arab Integration* report (2014) and *Towards Justice in the Arab World* report (2016), which was withdrawn by the UN secretary-general. She is a founding member of the International Association of Contemporary Iraqi Studies and cofounder of Tadhamun: Iraqi Women's Solidarity. She chairs the panel of judges for the Middle East Monitor Palestine Book Awards and writes a weekly column for the London newspaper *Al Quds Al Arabi* (Arab Jerusalem). She has published extensively; her publications are listed below.

Nonfiction in English:

City of Widows: An Iraqi Woman's Account of War and Resistance. New York: Seven Stories Press, 2008.

Dreaming of Baghdad, translation of *Fī awriqat al-dhākira* by the author, with Paul Hammond. New York: Women Unlimited, 2012. Also translated as *Through the Vast Halls of Memory.* Worcestershire, UK: Hourglass, 1991.

The Torturer in the Mirror with Ramsey Clark and Thomas Ehrlich Reifer. New York: Seven Stories Press, 2010.

Novels in Arabic:

Mafātīḥ madīna (Keys to a City). London: Dar al-Hikma, 2000.

Nisā' 'alā safar. London: Dar al-Hikma, 2001. Translated by Judy Cumberbatch, *Women on a Journey:*

Between Baghdad and London. Austin: Univ. Texas Press, 2007.

Short story collections in Arabic:

Bayt al-naml (The House of Ants). London: Dar al-Hikma, 1996.

Abʿad mimmā narā (Beyond Our Horizon). London: Dar al-Hikma, 1997.

Thammata ākhar (There Is Such Other). London: Dar al-Hikma, 1999.

Ḥayāt muʿallaba (Packaged Life). London: Dar al-Hikma, 2007.

She has been running writing workshops for Palestinian and Tunisian women prisoners since 2016, and to date three volumes of their writings have been published:

Ḥafla li-Thā'ira: Filastiniyyāt yaktubna al-ḥayāt (Party for Thaera: Palestinian Women Writing Life). London: e-Books, 2017.

Dafātir al-milḥ: Tūnisiyyāt ʿan tajribat al-sijn al-siyāsī (Journals of Salt: Tunisian Women on Political Imprisonment). Tunis: Kalima, 2019.

Banāt al-siyāsa: sardiyyāt munādilāt barskbaitīf (Political Daughters: Narratives of Perspectif Women Resistance Fighters). Tunis: Zanoobya, 2020.

Wen-chin Ouyang, FBA, is professor of Arabic and comparative literature at SOAS, University of London. Born in Taiwan and raised in Libya, she completed her BA in Arabic at Tripoli University and PhD in Middle Eastern Studies at Columbia University in New York City. She is the author of *Literary Criticism in Medieval Arabic-Islamic*

Culture: The Making of a Tradition (1997), *Poetics of Love in the Arabic Novel* (2012), and *Politics of Nostalgia in the Arabic Novel* (2013). She has also published widely on *The Thousand and One Nights*, often in comparison with classical and modern Arabic narrative traditions, European and Hollywood cinema, magic realism, and Chinese storytelling. She founded and co-edits *Edinburgh Studies in Classical Arabic Literature*. She has been the editor-in-chief of *Middle Eastern Literatures* since 2011. She also co-chairs the editorial committee of Legenda's *Studies in Comparative Literature*. She was a member of the judging panel for the Man Booker International Prize for Fiction from 2013 to 2015. She also judged the Saif Ghobash Banipal Literary Translation Prize in 2017. A native speaker of Arabic and Chinese, she has been working toward Arabic-Chinese comparative literary and cultural studies, including Silk Road Studies.

She has worked closely with *Banipal: Magazine of Modern Arab Literature* since its foundation in 1998 and has hosted and chaired many of their events with authors and translators. https://www.youtube.com/watch?v=6W3BtPG-eQ4

She also runs the Arabic Poetry and Stories in Translation workshops with Marina Warner at SOAS and Birkbeck. https://arabicstories.poetry.blog/